# Millennium Man, Volume 1:

# The Confessor

# Age: 995

**Millennium Man: Volume 1**
**The Confessor**

Copyright© 2015 Sean DeLauder

ISBN-10: 1514801337
ISBN-13: 978-1514801338

Book cover design by Sean DeLauder

For Laura,

who insisted

# CONTENTS

Those who cannot remember the past are condemned to repeat it.

—Santayana

# Prelude

I have never considered myself an evangelist, but I have become so. I do not think myself a demon, a monster, or some vile thing of nightmare fantasy, but such is what they call me. Many times I have said I do not believe. Based on experience. Based on fact. In a zealot-filled world I say it often, more and more frequently to none but myself. But one thing you will never hear me say: I do not recall.

The great curse upon humankind is that they forget, and as a consequence they repeat their atrocities over and over. I too have a curse, though many would call it a blessing. For a long time I also thought it a blessing, until the gift wasted itself time and again on those who needed it most. And as a consequence of that gift all the suffering I have witnessed, all the misery, all the malevolence, I carry with me in heart-grinding vividness. Forever.

In a world of self-perpetuating wickedness, of fear and cruelty, my curse is not that I forget, but that I remember.

DeLauder

# Yesterday

The city is not what it was.

The street I walk along stinks of the churning water from last night's rainfall, my bare feet slipping on the shifting sandbar of a mud-clogged gully. The rising sun heating my face will evaporate the shallowest rivulets, giving humid weight to the air, while leaving pools to stagnate. By evening, clouds of insects will hover in malevolent patches of biting smog, picking at withered bodies piled upon flatcarts after today's ceremony.

The city is a boneyard. All the soft tissues have long since turned to dust, leaving skeletal remains of caved-in buildings and loose footprints of crumbled roadways. Even more recent features, the low defensive wall ringing the city, a slumping heap of disintegrating vehicles and other debris which none understand and serves no purpose, have receded like ripples at the far edge of a puddle.

Each step is haunted by memory. I'm walking through the familiar remnants of a long-dead corpse, the gray and decaying form of something I once knew in full color.

As I make my way through the city to the morning service others emerge from the ruined buildings—a hodgepodge of mud and wood built into the eroding frameworks of stone and steel—and we flow together like the mealy water gurgling along sandy channels in the street. The air is an accumulation of pungent odors, of history no one detects, of people and ideas brought here to be victims of a massive, public homicide.

We trudge through oily puddles, passing the eroded remnants of the long past. Where most see low piles of rock I see the high archways of the Alcala Gate. They see a high platform of flat stone and I see where a bronze King Charles sat mounted in a place known as the Gate of the Sun. Where they smell the sour odor of unwashed bodies, I smell paella and tortilla, in the background of their murmurs and shuffling I hear the noise of hundreds of thousands of voices and vehicles. Where they see mud and decay and hollowed out shells, I see a city rich with history, of clear running water, of ancient fortresses, of genuine civil strife, a prize to be won.

Through an opening in a building's crumbled brick wall I see inhabitants scramble down debris ramped into a makeshift staircase. On the face of the structure, scarcely visible unless one knows where to look, I see the faded lettering embossed above a great mouth in the building: Parque de Bomberos.

Ahead, a mother herds her two children along to the town square. Dressed in the brown fabric common to everyone, her hair tied back with a piece of string pulled from her fraying garment.

"Come on then, little soldiers, we don't want to miss out, do we?" she asks.

"No!" replies one.

"Not a slice!" adds the other.

They scurry onward toward the great clearing and the wooden platform in the middle. One massive stone support was the pedestal for King Philip upon his steed. Here the Paterno will give his sermon and exercise the rites of the service and the Judicator will perform the duties of his office.

Many are already here. We pack into the plaza once called the Main Square, Plaza of the Constitution, and Marketplace of the Republic, among the crouched and humble structures. A low buzz issues from the crowd—the cumulative effect from thousands of tight whispers.

Banners on each corner of the stage hang limp in the morning doldrums. Some depict the holy stone streaking toward our impetuous and unrepentant planet. Another is of a Crusader crushing heathens of no particular denomination underfoot. The last image is that of a face. When the wind is strong the banners snap angrily, and the distorted face gesticulates at the crowd with demonic hostility, and the people hiss back at it.

Each time I see the face, it's eyes tiny and red, thin black lips pulled back over a villainous, leering grin, I have to smile. Because all the people standing around me, who shout and curse and hurl stones at that demonic visage, don't recognize the basis for that image standing amongst them. If they did, I wouldn't be here.

I am prying fingers, wells gone sour, scribbles of malcontent upon the alley walls. I am the one who pours sand on the scales of their conscience. I am the antithesis, the antichrist, the manifestation of evil in human form for the religious zealotry that has consumed humankind. I am like the vampire, or werewolf for the ignorant middle ages to which we have reverted, a collection of human fears balled into a convenient and terrifying

5

explanatory myth, forged in hell, sent here to corrupt, a taint upon thought that makes them impure. Each day I am purged through these ritual ceremonies.

The buzz of the crowd intensifies as the banners of the Order of the Illuminated appear at the outer edge of the crowd. The pair of white banners, with the emblem of a rectangular shield upon them. They are symbols of honor and repute. Those first shields used by the gang that now called itself the Order had been stripped out car doors, unwieldy but sturdy.

The Paterno arrives and mounts the stage, clad in a tan cloak and hood. Behind him is the Judicator, an enormous man by necessity who carries a great and horrifying axe of tremendous heft slung across both shoulders, the blade long and bright, the very air curling off in ribbons around it. Behind them two guards lead a shrouded man to a wooden pillory.

When the prisoner appears, the crowd erupts. They surge forward, the whole organism of the square contracting around the platform like a pumping heart. Their screams are unintelligible, filled with blind rage. No one knows the man, or no one claims to know him. He could be a wanderer from another compound, someone taken off the streets here, or a prisoner shipped home by the marauding Crusader army.

The shroud is jerked away and the prisoner in the pillory blinks in the morning light. He tries to stand, wriggle his arms in pathetic futility. He tries to pull his head out of the vise. When he can't he begins to panic. Looking across the crowd and finding no sympathetic faces, he begins to moan. Already they are screaming, and his words are lost amid the din of the crowd. But it is easy to read his mouth.

*What have I done? What is my crime?*

Truth be told, he probably hasn't done anything. *Save him*, you say. Or, more likely, you don't. There's no nobility left in humankind. So I don't save him.

A few days ago he probably stood in a similar crowd, jeering with the rest without knowing why, carried along like a broken branch caught in the rapids of a river of hatred. And over the course of the next ten minutes, as they carry out their crude rites, his cries reach the very heavens to which the roiling crowd will dedicate this ritual.

Monstrous, hypocritical creatures we have become.

The Paterno begins to speak and the crowd responds. Soon the Paterno is shouting, his voice faint much of the time, muted by distance and the accumulated noise of the yawping people. People cheer with every stroke of his fist, every time he points an accusing finger back to the man drooping in the wooden clamp, though I'm certain they can't hear what he's saying.

The frightened prisoner looks out across the acres of jeering courtyard, eyes wide with astoundment. He has seen this scene many times in reverse and searches the crowd with a sense of surreality for his own face, as though to confirm the dream.

The sermon ends and the crowd goes quiet. I can see in his face the recognition, the understanding of what is to happen next. His cries become shrill. He is moved to a long, wooden table and secured by his arms and legs. The straps are tightened and his appendages extend. Then the Judicator holds the tool

7

of his trade aloft, turning in place for all to see, the crowd thrilling at the glints of light on sharp metal, and sets it aside. They scream in delight, enjoying the prisoner's terror simply because it is not their own. Each day someone dies, and if one person dies for their sins, everyone else lives another day sinless.

At the same time, the Paterno moves to a smaller table arrayed with short, metal instruments. The prisoner can still rotate his head, and it follows the Paterno, gesticulating, no doubt pleading for his life. But to no avail.

The horrors humans visit upon one another are alien to me. I feel I am from a distant planet, marooned in a nightmare from which I'm unable to wake. Every day a sacrifice. Can a people sin so much that such measures are needed, or do these exercises simply satisfy a lust for cruelty?

"From dust," calls the Paterno, and the crowd completes the phrase with him, "to bloody dust we return."

The Paterno cuts and guts him, turning to hold ropy innards aloft with every new slice, while the crowd roars and the prisoner's cries for mercy become garbled and bubbly. At the apex of the display, the prisoner's energy and life all but exhausted, the Judicator concludes the ritual by hefting the symbolic tool of his office and ending the gurgling cries for help with a powerful downward chop that sinks the blade into the table and leaves the handle quivering.

The prisoner, the Paterno, and the stage drip with deep red gore that will harden in the sun, adding to the crisp mat covering the platform.

Senseless and horrifying as it appears, there is a purpose: fear. A generalized, medieval fear of everything. A ceaseless fear fed by the possibility that you may be apprehended at any moment, that you may be committing some atrocity without knowing, always worried you may be caught unwitting in some subtle transgression. And no one, no one resists. Why? No one asks—that may be the greatest tragedy of all. Curiosity and skepticism are murdered upon that platform, for to doubt the purpose of the executions is itself a sin worthy of death.

Questions are an indication of deviant thought. So out went universities and philosophy and science. The only trades that remain are those absolutely essential: tradesmen and apprentices; farmers and builders; most of which is determined by the infrastructure of the Order. Technology, that which wasn't deemed outright blasphemous, fell into disrepair because no one knew how it worked, how to repair it when it stopped working, how to fabricate pieces to replace the parts that broke. Artificial selection, a corollary effect of these executions, has bred people who don't ask questions, who believe what they are told is all they need to know.

Humanity has made a science of simplicity. Simplicity and specialization are what ensure survival. Government is a complicated machine, prone to error, human error—the worst kind. The beauty of theocracy is that humans are unaccountable. As such, there are no mistakes, no matter how large the catastrophe or strife. Errors in judgment, even when people die, are not attributable to humans. They are god's will. It is a solution that eliminates any sense of responsibility and leaves us free to explore the deepest depravities completely unfettered by guilt.

DeLauder

As the crowd disperses I remain, eyes fixed on the distorted caricature flapping in the breeze. Beyond it the clock face overlooking the town is locked between minutes, gears rusted together in a great toothed mass of brittle orange and green metal. And I return to a thought that visits more and more as the days peel away. That even though we all seem frozen in an era of celebrated brutality, that nothing moves forward or backward, that time itself seems broken, I am, nevertheless, running out of it.

It's as I think this that I feel a hand grip my shoulder and a baritone voice says *Come with us*, and I know it's my turn, and I say *Yes. Thank you. I've been waiting.*

# The Confessor

New straw crackled under Confessor Prado's feet as he followed the guard along the narrow walkway. Even so, the enclosure stank of urine and feces through the baggy sleeve he held to his face. The guards told him he'd grow accustomed to the stench. That was months ago. Vile and pitiful people filled the air with their rot. They disgusted him.

The cells of the judicatum wrapped around a great atrium of black space where the torchlight could not reach, and from this void echoed the ghostly voices of prisoners calling for salvation. To Confessor Prado they sounded like lost souls shouting from the darkness of the ether, the damned crying from purgatory, the doomed seeking absolution they did not deserve from a fate they earned. He did not look at them, but kept his eyes forward, striding past their cells in silence.

*Please, Confessor. There's been a misunderstanding. I was by the river taking in my nets. I had done nothing wrong.*

*Confessor, help me! I have a family in the dregs, my wife has no employ, my children starve. Soon they will be turned out into the streets…*

Their cries faded as he passed, melding into a steady, pleading cacophony. The general tone was of confusion and fright. But there was no misunderstanding. They were all here for a reason, chosen by the unerring hand of fate. They were all guilty. It was his job to help them determine why.

Torches jutted from emplacements along the walls, illuminating the path ahead, littered by faces pressed against the bars and a long row of arms waving at him like stinging tentacles. The walkway was just wide enough for him to stay beyond the reach of the hands clutching at his layered brown robes without bumping against the rough and rusted guardrails.

"He's this way, Confessor," said the guard over a shoulder, batting at the limbs reaching through the bars with a short wooden club. Arms and faces drew back momentarily, but their desperation made them forget the pain. "Be warned, he's not normal. A mischief maker at the least. Something more at the worst. Never done anything to hurt anyone, but he might be dangerous."

The guard stopped before a cell and reached for the thick metal ring porcupined by the spines of numberless iron keys. He looked at each one for a careful moment, then flipped to the next. As the guard searched for the proper key, Prado looked toward the cell, trying to penetrate the darkness. No arms stretched through the bars, nor did any cries for help. The cell appeared empty, and Prado almost asked if he'd been brought here in error when he saw something move at the outermost edge of the torchlight. Prado squinted, and after a moment he could make out a hand, drumming against the leg of a man seated in the darkness. As he continued to come into focus, Prado realized the man was facing him, with eyes pinched in amusement.

The prisoner was not large. Smaller than Prado, who joined the brotherhood long ago when it became apparent he would not grow enough to be useful in the army. With the opportunity to destroy heathens taken from him, Prado applied himself doubly to his career as Confessor, determined to wring the sinners from the nation if he could not help crush the non-Christo forces around the world.

"Almighty maker," muttered the guard.

The guard held the unfastened padlock in hand, a key poised above the hold to unlock the tumblers, then looked into the cell where the prisoner looked back with an expression of satisfaction.

"Did he do that?" asked Prado.

"Must have forgotten to fasten it, that's all," the guard replied. But even in the weak light Prado could see in his pallid face that he didn't believe it.

Strange the prisoner hadn't taken the opportunity to escape. Or rather, it was no surprise at all. For all their confusion and terror, no one tried to escape, held in place by the weight of their sins.

"Those doors," said the prisoner in a smooth, slow voice, "once opened by themselves. In a time when there was less and less cause for incarceration. Such a dramatic reversal. We are, in so many ways, at the opposite end of the spectrum, trapped in an aborted cycle."

"Shut your gob," said the guard, banging his club against the bars, then pulling the lock free and unwinding the chain that held the door shut.

The prisoner was not restrained, but remained seated on the concrete bench protruding from the wall, waiting as Prado ducked through the entry with the guard.

13

No prisoners needed to be restrained. No one dared attack a Confessor. That would mean certain damnation. And deep down, everyone here knew they were guilty, even if they didn't understand why just yet.

The man's eyes followed Prado as he entered. They were striking, even in the darkness, radiant with something Prado could not place. They probed and scrutinized. There was a wry distance to his expression, as though he saw things differently from how they were. His hair fell in waves to his shoulders, parted along the center. He was smiling, but the grooves running from the corners of his mouth framed his chin and gave him an appearance of disappointment.

"Would you like to begin?" the man asked.

Prado blinked, unsure how long he'd been staring, certain it had been too long.

"I told you to shut it!" said the guard.

He brandished the club and brought it down against the cement bench with a crack that made Prado jerk. As best he could tell, the man did not blink.

Prado did not answer. Instead, he unfolded a wooden chair and waved the guard away. The guard backed obediently out of the cell and refastened the padlock.

"You holler if he tries anything, right? Feel free to call out even if he doesn't. I'd be more than happy for a chance to knock that smirk off his face."

Prado waved his hand again and sat. The guard hesitated, the Prado heard the fading boot steps as the guard padded slowly away. The prisoner's eyes tracked the guard as he left, then shifted back to Prado. He grinned, always, the straight line of his mouth tilted up at one end, down at the other.

The man was lean and short, and appeared as old as himself. Perhaps in his mid-thirties. The customary robe most wore had been taken from him, leaving him with only a thin shirt and short pants. Food shortages made obesity obsolete in all the castes except the upper theocracy, but this man was not malnourished. His face was full and Prado could see cords of muscle flexing beneath the skin as his fingers drummed against his leg. Yet this was not what made him different from those who confessed to him before.

This one did not plead or apologize when Prado and the guard approached. He did not prostrate himself, or tug at Prado's robes, or wail in desperation to the deaf heavens. Instead, there was a uncanny sense of self assurance, of self righteousness he'd seen only in the High Masters—the High Masters of the Order of the Illuminated who conferred with the almighty and received instructions for the content of Paterno sermons, the number of wicked the Confessors should process, and where the Generos of the Crusader Armies should send their forces. This was not the face of the penitent. This was the face of defiance.

All the better to break him.

But who was this creature? A disgraced High Master, perhaps. Only a High Master would be so well fed and clever enough to unfasten the padlock without the key. Only a High Master would be so self assured, believing he could extricate himself from this situation through conversation. However, of all people, a High Master should know that was impossible.

When High Masters fell, which occurred on occasion, it usually came about as an abrupt and inexplicable loss of faith. Something in their mind jackknifed, folded up on itself, their thoughts flying along until they met an unbreachable wall. They suddenly came to believe they were trapped, or their actions unjustified, or that, unspeakably, the Maker whom they served did not hear nor speak to them, not because they lost the ability to speak to that higher plane, but because he simply was not there. These High Masters found themselves infected by powerful demons of confusion and doubt. Which made it all the more clear to Prado and everyone else how vigilant they must remain. Empty Throne Syndrome, it was called. It was, Prado felt, a form of insanity, to which the elderly often fell victim. Yet this man was by comparison quite young.

Maybe he was a demon, or some other wicked emissary of the Vitruvian devil. Only such a creature would revel in their guilt. Such a creature would possess supernatural powers, allowing it to magick the locks.

Discomfort wormed inside of Prado and he felt a thin sheen of anxious sweat on his brow. Not fear. Perhaps excitement. A challenge.

In all his experience he'd never met such a being, though almost all Confessors and Paternos had shared with him or a congregation a story of the strange workings they'd encountered in a world rife with these mischievous creatures. They were rumored to dwell in throngs underground or in underwater cities, able to manipulate the machines of the wicked past that consumed the souls of men to operate. At one time they proliferated in such numbers that the

Great Rock fell upon the planet, obliterating their kind in great numbers and returning the world to a state of virtue.

But if a devil or a cast down High Master, why would he remain once the lock was magicked? For that Prado had no answer.

"Good evening," said Prado. "I will be hearing your confession."

"Is that so?" the man responded. He straightened, as might a child in a game whose turn has come. "I was unaware I had anything to confess."

"Of course you have. I'm here to help you determine what that is, and allow you to go to the Maker with a clear conscience. Identifying and accepting your crimes against the Maker is the first step toward absolution."

"And the next?"

"Addressing the Maker in person."

The man smiled.

"I've no interest in meeting *your* maker." He leaned forward on his bench, eyes locked on Prado with an expression of amusement. "You have an irresponsible and childish maker, by my reckoning. I don't think we'd have much to talk about."

"Why do you say that?"

"Preventing us from being what we could is indicative of a bully. If there is a maker responsible, they should be ashamed. I don't believe a god has anything to do with it. No god would engage in such petty foolishness or so much vendetta. A god is wiser than this. A god did not waste a world as a means to crush our will to exist. This is what it is, we are what we are, because we failed a test."

The man's eyes scrolled across the bars behind Prado and he knew the guard has passed by, perhaps slowing to cast a malevolent glare into the cell. A series of slow clanks rang from behind as the guard dragged his club against the bars. Prado saw fading dark welts on the man's shoulders and neck and knew he'd been visited before.

Something about this man ruffled the guard. Perhaps he found the prisoner's lack of faith maddening. For the thoroughly indoctrinated, anyone who believed differently from themselves was incomprehensible.

The prisoner's defiance did make the confession interesting, free of the typical caterwauling and genuflection Prado usually experienced. Nevertheless, the conversation added color to the repetitive gray of the experience. It did not change his approach. Violence was not necessary. There would be no need to coerce a confession through physical duress. An abused man would say anything to end the pain. Above all else, a confession must be sincere. Otherwise, what was the point?

The difference in temperament in this guard from others is what made him a guard at a detention facility rather than a soldier in the Crusader army, and Prado a fourth-ranked Confessor of the Order rather than street vermin shouting "Holy holy!" like some obnoxious evangelist at everyone who walked past. Some men were urgent and hasty. Not Prado. He knew guilt and worry would wear through this façade like drops of water drilling patiently through a block of stone. It always did.

The guard was correct, though. This man had proven different from the others. Most men and women pled for release, offering trivial transgressions as they searched themselves for the true reason for their arrest. That none existed made the search all the more interesting, and penetrating. Most times they dug so deep they did find something in themselves that made them believe they deserved to be here. That was the goal.

"I agree,' said Prado. "Humankind failed a test of pride. We were punished. Now we are healing."

The prisoner shook his head in negation.

"Humanity failed a test of humanity. And we continue picking at the scab."

Quite the labyrinth the man had built around his guilt. Nevertheless, maze would mean nothing when its walls eroded. Again. All it took was an erosion of hope and time. All things in time.

"What is your name?" asked Prado. "So I might address you properly."

The prisoner's smile faded.

"My name? My true name? It's been a long time. So long it dangles on the edge of my memory. And remembering is my purpose. Isn't that strange?"

Prado leaned back in his chair and drew a pipe from his cloak. He heard the guard stiffen against the bars and take a sharp pull of breath. Tobacco appeared only in the hands of the truly favored. Few places within reach of the Holy Order produced it. The elite rarely smoked in the presence of plebes, lesser tradesmen, or prison guards, let alone in the presence of a prisoner. Prado didn't much care for those unspoken rules. The only thing that mattered was whether he secured a confession. And he always did. The prisoner watched Prado pack tobacco in the bowl and strike sparks against a flint.

"Curious habit," he said. "Dangerous."

"Perhaps. So long as I continue my work in just and appropriate fashion, I am protected by a vaunted power."

"Oh no," laughed the prisoner. "If there's one thing the various almighties frown upon is indulgences and a false sense of invulnerability. They dislike hubris. No one likes a snob."

Prado blew out a large cloud of smoke.

"Have you remembered?" he asked.

"What is *your* name," countered the man. "If I may ask."

"Prado," Prado responded. "Alejandro Prado. Confessor, fourth rank. I am thirty-four years old. I have two children. Boys. Recruited five years ago to serve in the Crusader Army. I am sure they are quite large by now. They will be great heroes. Of this I have little doubt. And I have nothing to hide and nothing for which I am ashamed."

"Young, aren't you? For a fourth-rank Confessor. Well in line to be a High Master one day. I'm glad it's you they sent. Very glad. An influential man such as yourself could have a very long reach in the future."

"And your name?"

"Thomas," answered the prisoner. "Thomas Manu. A long time ago that might have meant something to someone. My parents. My first wife. My first friends. But I've had more familiar names since. Names you would recognize."

Prado removed the pipe and cleared his throat.

"Shall we begin, then?"

"With a confession? No. No, I don't feel I've anything of interest to confess. Nothing you haven't heard countless times already. Sins of the flesh, sins of pride. Everyone has those. Even you, I'm sure. You must if you have children. Your hypocrisies are what have saved us from extinction. I'd rather tell you about myself. About my history."

"The past is where your most shameful sins lie," said Prado.

Thomas shrugged.

"Do you know why the world ended?" he asked.

"It has not ended," said Prado. "You and I are still here, are we not?"

"Fair enough. Do you know why it stopped, then?"

"If you're referring to the disaster, the fallen stone, and the rebirth of society, that is simple. We lost faith."

Thomas jabbed a finger in the air.

"Yes! Just as you say, but not as you think. We lost faith in ourselves. Once we lose faith in ourselves we put our faith elsewhere, and we cease creating solutions and holding ourselves accountable for our failures. So not only did we fail a test, we failed to learn a lesson from our failure. That makes it doubly embarrassing."

Prado sighed.

"I am not here for a lesson in history or philosophy. Both are well understood."

"No. It's why *I* am here."

A demon, Prado thought. So sure of its delusion because it wanted to convince Prado as well. It raised interesting questions. From where did this demon, and others, originate? What did it intend? What motivated its desire for corruption?

He understood, from all previous reports, that demons behaved as did this man. Demons spoke in riddles. They avoided questions by asking their own. And rather than focus upon its own guilt, it chose to focus on yours, attempting to revers the role of prisoner and confessor. But there were ways to make even demons play by the rules.

"You understand I can eschew this confession," said Prado. "I am here for you, not the other way around."

"That's where you're wrong," Thomas interjected. "I'm here for you. I'm here for everyone."

"Why is that?"

"Because they forget."

"And you do not?"

"No. I don't."

Prado took a long pull on his pipe and blew out a long plume of smoke that settled over Thomas. He did not cough or blink or rub his eyes. He simply stared intently, imploringly, at Prado, trying to discern the effect of his words.

"You can go to the scaffold without any opportunity to purge yourself of any burdensome secrets. You can choose to end with your soul in a state of desolation. I'd much rather hear your history than your perception of society."

Prado crossed one leg over the other and invited Thomas to continue with a wave of his hand.

"Good," said Thomas.

He leaned back against the wall and disappeared into the shadows. His voice emanated from the darkness and it seemed to Prado as though he was audience to the storytelling of a neglected and dusty power, recovered from a millennia of isolation. The voice was wistful and heavy with remorse.

"Memories seem recent as a yesterday," said Thomas, "still vibrant and fresh, as if I could go back home and find everyone waiting to resume their daily trivialities, just gears waiting for a crank. Each time I pass something I remember, a house, a monument, a factory, a university, now a military stronghold, a church, or a pile of dust, it jars. It confuses. I understand time has passed and change has occurred, yet there's still a sense of being stuck in time. My oldest memories are my foundation, far below the surface now, covered over with hundreds of feet of detritus. I find it sad. Sad in a way no one understands any longer because no one else remembers, nor cares to. There's no basis for comparison, which makes it easy to get lost in the uniformity of indoctrinated mediocrity. So. Let us return to a yesterday. A foundation that will allow us to see the deterioration, the waste, the loss, all layered upon one another reaching up and up over time bringing us to now. That seems the best place to start. So. We begin again."

DeLauder

# The Program

My first memories are of the stars.

Over the long years they never change. At least, not that I can detect. Yet I never tire of them the way I have of other things. They take longer to wear away, I suppose. Popular fads came and went, only to come and go again. For a long while after the disaster that brought us to what we are now only the brightest were visible through the heavy clouds of debris. Years and years passed before breezes brushed back the great billows to reveal the plane of our brilliant galaxy—that channel of stars splitting the night like a seam where the two halves of the universe joined around us. It's interesting to think when we lost sight of the stars we lost sight of our ambitions as well. Like ancient mariners beneath a cloud-covered sky, we wandered.

But the stars returned, in time.

When I was young a cloudless sky looked deepest blue in daylight, and at night faint lights shone down from billions of points along the outer sphere like distant keyholes. Just as now. I dreamt of ways to explore the vastness overhead and how to survive the long spaces between destinations. It was a common dream then.

Though I was a boy, I remember those moments with great clarity. That, of course, is why I was chosen for the experiment. Because I remember.

Since my childhood, light from Proxima Centauri has traveled from our sun, and that light from our sun shone back, one hundred and twenty-five times. I've seen three hundred and fifty thousand suns, and on dull gray days I think I can sense its boredom with us. When I look up now I can see Fomalhaut or Vega or Epsilon Eridani, and think we might almost be there, exploring their satellites. I imagine the contrails from our machines crossing the skies and sometimes fool myself into thinking a wisp of cloud is a hint that they have returned. But my searches always end in vain.

You aren't certain what I'm saying, of course. You don't have the breadth of experience. I see slivers of puzzlement winking through cracks in your calm exterior. Oh, you're very controlled, but I can see you trying to understand, I can see curiosity gnawing upon you, and something deep down, a leap of intuition perhaps, might give your suspicions greater weight. Curiosity can be controlled, but there will always exist a yearning for understanding, such as what you seek now, and that is why this cannot last forever.

In my earliest days our ambitions drove us toward conclusions that years before we might never have thought possible. Fissures developed in the shells of problems some believed could never be unlocked; light showed beneath doors long dark, where 500 years prior we allowed their mysteries to be explained by magick and mysticism, and a host of other absurdities we shattered like glass idols against our understanding. We could hear the distant click of tumblers in locks and the creak of hinges as the cosmos opened to us. We were masters of technology, had created computing machines more powerful than our own minds, could manipulate our own genome, had harnessed the basics of matter transfer, and even slowed dramatically the degradation of our bodies. Our horizons extended to the edge of our most fanciful dreams.

Now your eyes widen. You suspect the rumors of the past, which seemed scarcely believable, even as you heard them again and again as part of parable and myth, and wonder if they might have more than a few specks of truth to them.

Perhaps a few mythical humans may spring to mind: Abraham, Gilgamesh, Mithras. It was said they lived hundreds of years, established or ruled many tribes of humankind, much as your warring leaders do now. But no, your histories no longer reach back that far. Your creation myths are appallingly shortsighted, even if those stories have been recreated over again, just as they were created and repeated and borrowed by one another before. But you have heard rumors of those with uncommon long life. Eerie and unsettling tales of human who appear again and again over vast spaces of time, apparently gifted with uncommon long life. A gift not from some almighty, but something they gave themselves. From dust we came and to dust we shall return, and from that dust we shall make ourselves anew. In your haste and ignorance you labeled them demons and corruptors, blamed them for any ills that have befallen you, used their purported influence as justification to persecute others.

You do this because you are afraid, because you don't understand. It is natural to fear what is not understood. It is foolish to use the unknown and unproven to chastise others. This is a sin against your very humanity. But how can you know better when you know no alternative? How can you know the alternative without a teacher?

27

DeLauder

It so happens that you're in luck. Once, many years before, teaching was my profession.

* * *

When I was twenty-seven years old I was selected for the program. For my excellent health, my disease-free pedigree, and, of course, because of my memory. I remember many things. Not everything, but most things. I don't remember the placing of every grain of a sandy beach, nor every dot on a freckled girl's face. I do, however, recall most of them.

It was a blessing then. So much to learn. It didn't occur to me there would be so many things I would want to forget.

Consider it a mercy that you forget. All the ones you love who are lost, the experiences that sting, the wounds that knit seamlessly together—over time the images fade, the ridges they clove in the landscape of your heart slowly erode. Not so with me. The grief remains vivid and close, accessible at any time in a library of experiences. It motivates.

Even though I could see the changes occurring in humanity at the time of the great disaster, the planetfall, rather *we*, the others and I could see the change, we were powerless to stop it. In time, it destroyed many of us. But I've escaped. So far.

But I digress. I apologize. My memory is everywhere at once, so it is easily distracted.

Yes. The program. It wasn't simply called the program, of course. Like so many things it had a number of names. People were far more numerous and far more

28

imaginative. The Continuum. Humanus Infinitus. The Journeyman Project. On and on. Every nation, every religion, every ethnicity had its own name. Those involved called it TVM, or The Vitruvian Man.

Ah, that's a name you've heard before. I can see it in the roundness of your eyes and the way your fingers grip your robes.

But what need for such a program? That's simple. In fact, the current situation is a perfect example of its necessity.

Human existence is no more than a flint spark of time. In that time, before we can do anything, we need to relearn everything those before us learned. Every generation, over and over and over again. Relearning the same information, making the same mistakes, again and again. To read human history is an exercise in exasperation and repetition. War, then peace, then war, then peace. Exploitation, then recovery, then exploitation again. Growth then regression. Prosperity then destitution. It was as if someone were standing on the coattails of progress, and every step forward required monumental effort from the greatest, most influential minds, for many existed with the sole purpose of resisting because they profited from a war, an inequality, or ignorance.

But what if the brevity of existence was removed? What if we only had to learn something once, remember the consequences and information and recognize patterns? What if we could travel to the stars ourselves rather than leave it to generations later, born into a mission that would last hundreds, maybe thousands of years?

When the representatives of the program first approached me, I was teaching classes at the University of Dartmouth. More than pragmatic trades, such as cobbling or carpentry. History, Literature, Biology, Physics, Astronomy, Chemistry. Not unlike your Masters teach rhetoric and dogma and interrogation at your schools. It wasn't because I was particularly brilliant or a polymath, but I remembered everything I'd been taught and was able to re-teach what I'd learned.

Of course, I had never heard of the program, and few would.

# 985 Years Ago

Two men arrived at the planetarium in the middle of a class. One never spoke his name, so I don't know it. I spotted them, interrupting the darkness with an open door and silhouetted against a square of light like ushers to some portal leading out of the universe.

Impolite. That was my first impression.

"To the north we have the caterwaul nebula. Look at it glow amongst the otherwise abundant darkness, a distraction and a nuisance."

The lights clicked on and abruptly the spell I had cast upon the classroom shattered. With that trigger, most students stood and headed to the exits, followed soon after by those who had awakened with the lights. The class ended, twenty minutes early.

Annoyed, I marched up the aisle to confront the men. They had already started and met me halfway.

"Did you learn anything?" I asked.

"Nothing more than we already knew," said the man whose name I would learn. The other, as he always would, remained silent.

"And what do I call you?"

"You may call me Hermes," he said.

"Messenger for the gods, eh? I have a message for them. Tell Apollo to keep his hands off the light switches. I'm in control of the cosmos here."

"And gift giver to the mortals."

"Did you get that? Do you take verbal messages or do I have to send a letter? How much is postage?"

Hermes absorbed my sardonic remarks unmoved. The other man seemed bored by my tirade, as though it kept them from some other chore. It became clear they felt no regret and I could do nothing but blunt my wit against them.

"What do you want?" I asked at last.

"Come with us," said Hermes, "and we'll show you. We have a position for you."

"I have a job," I responded as tartly as I could.

"Not a job," said Hermes. "A position. A role. A gift."

Hermes and his partner turned and headed back up the aisle. Infuriated by the vagaries and by my own curiosity, I struggled to resist, to turn away and prepare for the next class. Intrigue, as ever, proved triumphant.

I spotted them at a street running by the planetarium. Hermes entered the back seat of an inconspicuous gray vehicle. The other strode around to the driver's seat. Apart from their suits and demeanor, it struck me as odd. They had the attitude of government functionaries, protecting something, and yet they traveled in a gray sports utility vehicle like a mother carting her toddling children about on errands. It began to occur to me that a truly secret organization was not invisible, but transparent. Here they stood in broad daylight, yet no one saw them but me—a trait I've since adopted and has served me quite well.

Impulsively, I knew I was supposed to join them. I did. Pulled open the back door and slid onto the bench seat beside Hermes, who did not appear the least bit surprised.

"Let's go," he said.

The driver activated the vehicle and it leapt forward eagerly with a faint squeal from the tires.

"What gift," I asked.

"The most valuable commodity of all. With it, all things are possible."

*Faith.*

*No, Confessor. Not faith. It's time.*

DeLauder

# Foundation

The vehicle arrived before a large, pyramid-shaped building jutting several stories above ground, a mixture of gray cement and long lines of glass windows that wrapped around the structure like thick straps meant to prevent it from exploding. It bulged and towered, and I wondered at its purpose, what secrets hid within, though my initial observation proved rather banal.

"It's big," I said.

"Is it?" asked Hermes.

I had the impression he was making fun of my ignorance or understatement. A chuckle from the other recruiter confirmed my suspicion.

Hermes exited the vehicle and headed up the single walkway leading to the building, beckoning me to follow. I hurried out, not waiting for the other recruiter to open the door for me. The doors seemed an absurd distance from the street and I wondered why they would devote so much of their property to empty landscaping. But for the grass and the building, the enormous lot was blank.

My guide moved forward at a brisk pace and I kept up. When we reached the doors he turned, smiling, unbothered by the pace or distance or the brutal summer sun.

"Enter," he said.

The doors parted, washing me with a breeze of welcome cool air. I wiped a sleeve against my damp forehead and stepped inside.

Like the outside, the inside proved all but empty. The filtered sun murmured through the glass ceiling and great fans turned overhead, but the majority of what I could see was empty. People walked here and there in ties and dresses and button-down shirts pressed stiff and lineless, but I could not see where they were going or what they were doing. Several entered elevators, which lined the outer wall in numbers I'd never seen before. They puzzled me for a reason I could not understand, just for a moment, then I had it.

I looked up. The pyramid shape left nowhere for the elevators to go.

"Where do the elevators take people?" I asked.

I had no trouble guessing, but I didn't yet possess the imagination required to believe.

"Let me show you," said Hermes.

We entered and Hermes pressed a button. One set of doors closed, then a clear set behind them. For an instant, the second set of doors made no sense to me. That confusion didn't last long. I felt the elevator move. Not up. Down. And the space below the pyramid structure above appeared through those glass doors.

"Holy Christ!"

*Who?*

*Yes. There have been others before your Sky King and his emissaries. Christ was once a much more notable son of God. But many came before and receded into obscurity. It's a compelling tale we repeat over and over again.*

The lower floors opened into a hollow cylinder where the walls were marked by level after level of rings. People followed the walkways leading around the great circles, in white coats, in military uniform, in business attire, in full-body chemical suits.

Several areas had clear walls, and within them I could see the experiments conducted within. A faint point of light showed behind a heavily darkened window, then glowed until the window turned bright white before fading again. I saw a flash in one room, then another several rooms away, and wondered if the two had some connection. Near the top circle I saw a sign that read Accelerator Analysis, and realized the entire complex was used as a particle accelerator, particles coiling downward until they reached the final loop at the bottom floor.

In time I learned about many of these experiments. I came to utilize several of them, and still do to this day.

We descended ten floors before coming to a halt, and still several floors extended into the darkness below. I stared, my face pressed against the glass, until I felt a hand on my arm.

"Come along," said Hermes. "You'll have plenty of time after."

He drew me out the back of the elevator and into the ring where I could look up along the ribs of other floors. He dragged me along, mouth open and eyes everywhere but where I was headed, maneuvering upstream through other walkers who skirted wide around us to avoid being trod upon. I was not large, but I was oblivious, and, as I've learned, that can prove as damaging.

"What is this place?"

"It is exactly what it pretends to be. The Foundation. A non-profit that funds pure research. Far more, however, than we lead the public to believe. Better to avoid exploitation. We find the brightest, the most innovative, and we bring them here. There's no incentive for profit, and no boundaries but those placed upon you by a higher power." Hermes tapped a finger against his forehead. Then he fluttered a hand at the ceiling, dismissively. "Out there the geniuses of the world invent foibles for amusement: a telephone, a watch, a faster car, a taller building, a larger television, a clumsy robot, a simpler lifestyle. Here we make dabble with things that will matter: fusion energy, teleportation, quantum entanglement, faster-than-light travel."

He pointed to different areas of the structure as he named their pursuits, though none were visible. I found his assertions dubious, though his even-headed enthusiasm seemed scarcely under control. Beneath the majesty and serenity of that cool-minded man an eruption broiled just under the surface, and I found that excitement contagious, the first link in a chain, even against my best judgment. Should his calm exterior vaporize, mine would follow soon after. I did not fully grasp everything they were doing here, but I knew I wanted to know and that I wanted to be here.

"None of that is possible," I said, wondering how he would respond to the negativity.

Immune.

"Not quite, no. But not quite is just around the corner from absolutely."

"I'm no scientist. Why am I here? I have a good memory, and I can teach, but that's…"

Hermes stopped.

"Yes. Exactly. That has some very prominent uses as well. Are you familiar with Da Vinci's Vitruvian Man?"

*You stiffen, Confessor. That name has come to symbolize everything you despise. Yet you have no idea what it means.*

"Of course. A man of perfect proportion."

We passed through a door and into what appeared to be the waiting room of a doctor's office. He waved a hand to a receptionist behind a desk and window who leaned over to press a hidden button. A door leading deeper into the office buzzed as the lock released and we continued onward.

"The perfect man," said Hermes. "The ideal man. An infinite man. That's who we're looking for. But it's not someone we'll find."

Doors passed on both sides of a broad corridor until Hermes stopped before one of the identical doors and pushed it open with the fluidity of expectation. I looked back to see how many he'd passed and wondered how he'd known one from another of the unlabeled openings. The corridor curved over a horizon of blank doors and white walls beyond which I could not see. I looked ahead and saw the same. Then I looked at the door he'd selected for any distinguishing marks. Nothing.

"There are, I assure you, more interesting things here than the door," said Hermes.

I entered.

"So I'm the perfect man."

Hermes smiled.

"No. Of course not." He gestured to a table, so I turned and sat atop it. "But we can make you so."

Now I began to have a better understanding of the situation. I was not a scientist, and certainly not of the caliber employed here. I would not be making new discoveries or probing great mysteries. I was the experiment.

A nurse entered the room pushing a tray whose contents I paid little attention. Instead, I listened to Hermes, assuming they would draw blood samples or do some preliminary physical examination.

"What if we didn't have to repeat the errors of the past?" he mused. "What if someone remembered it? What if someone who remembered could advise in times of familiar crisis?"

The nurse rolled up my sleeve and rubbed and alcohol patch on my shoulder. A strange place for a blood sample, but Hermes had engaged my mind, taking my focus elsewhere. Needles never bothered me. They were a necessity to avert illness, examine my biochemistry, or aid someone else who might need a transfusion.

"What makes you think anyone would heed that advice?"

"A few successful prognostications is all that would be necessary."

"You have very little understanding of the human need for a sense, no matter how false, of free will and independence. No one likes being told what to do. We like screwing up. We like mistakes. We're very good at it."

The needle penetrated into my shoulder and I felt an eruption of pain. As I turned I saw the plunger hit the bottom of the barrel and the last remnants of a silver liquid disappear into the needle. The needle withdrew, the nurse capped it and dropped it into a biohazard container.

I clutched my shoulder and my mouth opened in a silent, stifled scream. I had never been stabbed before, though I have since, and I daresay the experiences were comparable. The pain drove straight to the bone and I felt the reverberations of that pain echoing through my body.

"We have been watching you for some time," said Hermes, "deciding if you were the correct person for this procedure."

Even though my eyes clenched from the pain I seem to recall him, moving to the rolling cart, observing the readout on the unidentified piece of machinery with satisfaction, then saying "this will help," and flipping a switch.

Immediately the pain ceased.

"That was *not* a blood draw."

"No," Hermes confirmed. "We already had plenty of samples."

"What, then?"

"A test."

"What kind of test?"

Hermes did not answer immediately. Instead he gazed at his watch. Only after a few moments did he return his attention to me.

"To see that you survived. To ensure the nanites did not attack other components of your body. It's possible your body can still respond negatively, in which case they will defend themselves, but the symptoms won't show for a few more days, and besides, our trials showed no ill effects."

"Nanites? You put nanites in me?"

"Nanites. Painful, yes. They work quickly, however, so the needle damage was repaired soon after they were activated."

Initially I was horrified. Knowing millions of tiny robots were scurrying through me made me want to peel my skin back and shake them out like bugs from a filthy blanket, but I soon realized the futility of complaining.

"You couldn't have given me a pill?"

"Your digestive system would have destroyed them. No, it was this or a suppository. The pain would have been the similar, though different in a geographical sense. We thought we would spare you that indignity. You're welcome."

Looking back I can recall my amazement, my excitement, yet at the same time I felt violated, as though a decision about myself had been made without me. We still cling to that, even though many attempts have been made to drive it out. A need for self determination, even in the smallest things. We want to believe we are in control of ourselves, even when we know our choices are limited to the point that we have no control.

"Still," Hermes continued. "That is only the first stage of the test. We have to make sure it worked."

The nurse produced a scalpel. Without a word, he made a long incision in my forearm. Blood welled immediately from the wound and through the fingers as I clenched my hand around it to staunch the flow.

I yowled, predictably, but Hermes and the nurse did not react. They watched the wound. And so, certain my cries and horror meant nothing to them, did I, wondering what they hoped to gain from my death.

Blood continued to seep through the long slice, but at a far slower pace than I expected. It had darkened considerably in the few moments after the cut and took on a faint silver hue. Then the blood stopped. Without staunching. Without a bandage.

The nurse approached again, tentatively, and I let him wipe the blood away with a moist gauze pad. Beneath the blood the skin was unbroken. No tears, no cut, no clotting. No indication that any damage had occurred.

"What have you done to me?" I asked.

"The nanites will repair any damage that occurs to your body. Cuts, scrapes, broken bones. They will even correct degraded vision, clean out infections and viruses, identify and reverse disease., slow the degradation of telomeres. Quite a marvel. They will add years to your life, we imagine."

"Why? You never asked if I wanted to be part of this. Never explained what this was."

Hermes remained unruffled, as though he'd anticipated these questions.

"We've watched you long enough to know. If you did not wish to participate, we would not have brought you here. Our interview was observation."

"Sounds more like self-fulfilling prophecy."

"We can reverse the treatment if you like."

"How?"

Hermes' expression remained fixed and impassive, but Thomas heard a lilt of amusement in his voice.

"Electrocution."

"And what are the penalties to having these nanites? Will I go crazy? Will they tinker with my brain?"

"An increase in appetite, certainly. You're consuming not just for yourself, but for your repair crew. Keep yourself fed and you will keep them functioning. Don't feed yourself and they may begin to feed on you."

One thousand years was their guess at my new lifespan, provided I received no maintenance. One thousand years to aid humanity, to watch it bloom into something brilliant, something extraordinary, something galactic in scale.

Don't get me wrong. I can be killed. I can starve. Many times I thought I might. Cut my head off and I won't grow another. I know. I saw the others killed. Grisly, horrible, public deaths. Mindless, brutal, vindictive. We have returned willingly to the dark ages. People have become witch hunters, gluttonous for violence, turning against one another to spare themselves, delighting in the suffering they inflict, despite knowing they might be the next victim. Far cries from the paradise and plenty promised by Hermes and the others of the Foundation.

Despite what your prognosticators state, the future is unpredictable. So the world changed, faster than I could teach it the perils of doing so. A calamity took us by surprise. The asteroid that struck us, silent and dark in its invisible approach, and from that countless more calamities arose.

Always I survive. Through every disaster. Always, to begin again. It's as if your almighty has a purpose for me.

# A Broken Millennium

Despite my age I seem little different from the day of the procedure. As you can see, there are a few gray patches in my hair, when the popular trend permits hair, and the skin is pinched at the corners of my eyes. Some things the nanites neglect, I suppose, but I won't complain.

For one hundred years I was a symbol, a triumph of human achievement. My existence was proof of supreme human intellect, granted an eidetic memory by chance and unnatural long life through scientific force, I bridged generations, served as arbiter of disagreements I'd seen before, warned against those I saw reemerging. Humanity trusted me; trusted us.

I stood in the open doorway leading to accomplishments long believed unimaginable, staring into the white light beyond. We were masters of our world, of ourselves, and our fate. We had opened Pandora's box and conquered the evils that issued forth, leaving our horizons limitless. Or so we thought. Then came the disaster. For almost 900 years since, I have been the enemy, a yardstick against which people measure their hatred. I am an abomination.

I am the symbol of technology, of science, of humankind trying to wrest control of its destiny from the divinity that arranged it. Does that sound familiar? I am the hunter of untempered souls, the whisper of doubt.

DeLauder

The Vitruvian Man is what they called me. A perfection of proportion, the triumph of the human mind personified. It was long a title of respect and dignity. Now it is the name with which your religions refer to me with such rancor.

After many years people forgot my real name, as most people do, and remembered the symbol only. After the disaster people hated me because I represented the element of humanity that had failed to protect them. I became an evil as part of an effort to vilify the accomplishments of the past. Just as the angels of the old religions become the devils of the new, I became The Vitruvian. Over time people forgot the other names for devil—Lucifer, Scratch, Old Nick, and variety of colloquial villains—leaving only me. I am the sole remaining devil in what was once a pantheon.

In truth, I consider myself more of a living document. I see and remember and warn. As I did then, so I do now. I wasn't wise enough then, hadn't been around long enough to see how the world would change, how humanity would change, so the counsel I offered proved ineffective. We were counseling the wrong people. But now I understand what to do. I know how to reverse what has happened to us.

How, you ask? To whom should I speak? It should be obvious. This time it is you.

# The Vitruvian Mission

Prado sat in his chair, arms huddled around his elbows, a thin column of gray smoke issuing from the pipe that had long since burnt out.

In all likelihood the man was lying, trying to unnerve him. To what end, Prado did not know. If this man were a demon the story could be explained as malevolent and mischievous. A test of his faith.

Prado did not believe in demons. Until now they struck him as mere fancy meant to terrify the addle-minded masses into fearing retribution for listening to the whispers of temptation. He's seen men and women go mad, though not as the consequence of hosting a vaporous creature with no other purpose than to cause discord and havoc. The world was a hard place and sanity often a luxury the lower orders struggled to maintain. Threats abounded: starvation, assault, illness, injury. Not to mention the danger of being apprehended by the White Vigil, a police force filled with those too undisciplined to be trusted in the army.

Now, with this self-certain being seated before him, asserting knowledge of a past no one could know and implying a falsehood about their origins, he wasn't so sure. Prado felt a horrifying nibble of doubt, of wonder, yet he did not let it control him. Faith had the power to crush doubt, to ignore what must be ignored in order to maintain that faith, and it sharpened his religious fervor to a still finer point.

He scowled, biting down on his pipe. This man, creature, or incarnation of malevolence, was a threat to their entire society.

"So you are the Vitruvian," said Prado, spitting the last word as though it left a bad flavor. "The Vitruvian Man. The Voice from the Past. The Devil's Hand. Ahriman. Asmodius. God of Blackness. The Adversary."

Thomas' eyes wandered, nodding while Prado rattled off the old names. There was a spectacular sense of aloofness about him. A maddening fearlessness that made Prado want to wrap his hands about Thomas' throat and strangle him. A man without fear was not humble. A man without fear was disrespectful, and would not only be denied admission into the Overworld Kingdom, but would corrupt and drag others down.

"Lamdonim, Illuminati," he added. "Yes, yes. I am. So many names for the same thing suggests an unhealthy preoccupation."

"And you are over eight hundred years old, a remnant of the previous age, the symbol of humanity's transgressions."

"More than nine hundred, and I am no symbol of transgression any more than you are a representative of divinity. You see the past through a distorted, broken lens, without any historical basis whatsoever. Your self-righteousness is far more misplaced, and dangerous, than mine. Mine is, at the least, has a foundation in the bedrock of fact."

Prado jerked to his feet, angrily. Walked to the cell bars. Stared into the blackness where a few whimpering voices stretched for his ears. None had ever proven so defiant and insistent upon the falsehood of his faith. It agitated him because

48

where Thomas had a history that sounded real Prado had only the myths upon which history was built. Arguing fact with faith and vice versa was a losing battle because they were weapons that had no effect on the other. The victor would not be the person who was right, but the person with greater belief in a position and the stamina to withstand a prolonged assault. He returned to his seat and sat.

"It bothers you?" asked Thomas.

"It's a myth," Prado answered, but it did bother him. The mere mention of the Vitruvian Man, and all he stood for, or rather stood against, caused the blood to thunder through his veins.

"What is religion but a standardized and living myth? Religions become myths when people stop believing them."

"Even though I know you are lying," Prado continued. "Even though I know you are mad, the very idea cloys at me. If it were true… If it were true, I would let the guards in with their clubs and their dogs to tear you apart."

"That would be a sin," Thomas pointed out. Then murmured, "without the proper public ritual. Do I speak like a mad man?"

Prado forced a short barking laugh.

"You're a very old man, Thomas. One way or another, your thousand years is coming to a close."

Thomas leaned back in his chair and for the moment his confidence ebbed.

"It is, yes. I know. I can sense it. There are some things, not important things, but something I can't quite recall that I'm sure I could not long ago. Have I been snared by the same erosion that overcomes everyone in time?

49

Maybe. Maybe this is just an unforeseen effect of extreme long life. I enjoy hearing my old name, though. Thank you. It's... full of old memory."

Hints of plausibility leaked through the story, as blood seeps through a bandage. Thomas seemed certain, and that made him convincing. But mad men believed everything they said, to the utmost absurdity. Still, so long as he continued speaking he may eventually come to the present, to his true lifespan rather than this imaginary, albeit entertaining past. And through that Prado would have his confession.

"Tell me, then," said Prado. "What have you learned in your many hundreds of years?"

Thomas grinned, mischievously, as though at some hidden piece of knowledge.

"What have I learned?" Thomas asked himself, bemusedly, then repeated. "What have I learned? I have learned you never stop learning. I learned terror has a cruel habit of muting all other emotions, and people succumb to terror very easily. I remember realizing how much I loved and missed my second wife, fifty years after she was gone. She was one of the last people who listened to me and my 'infinity of memory' as she called it. I have learned that obedience is simpler than thinking for oneself. To hate, blindly and recklessly, is simpler than taking the time to understand what makes someone different. I have learned it is easier to create a community joined by a common enemy than a cause. I have learned that one cannot rely upon hope alone—one must persevere."

Prado stared at Thomas, puzzling. What was the purpose of this charade? What did he seek to gain through it? There were those who sought nothing more than to be disruptive. They stood on the street corners and howled disjointed and incoherent noise about the end of days or the glory of the heavens, or any of a thousand repeated themes. This was more structured. More urgent. It had purpose.

"What is it you want?"

"To succeed," Thomas replied. "I've tried many times before, but each time I've been thwarted. Tragically. Each time there has been a choice, and each time you have chosen to sacrifice your humanity. Each time you have lost a bit of yourselves. That is the sacrifice you make to remain like this. I wonder sometimes how much remains to be salvaged, but I believe you can be saved. And through you, others."

Prado sighed.

"You must renounce what you have said. You must tell me you are not this… Vitruvian. Forget this absurd fantasy."

"Why? Because the idea of my existence bothers you? If anything, it should serve as confirmation that some of your tenets are true. If I have done anything, it has only been to disrupt this ruin you call a society. And I would never lie to you. Oh, the men and women who founded this great theocracy, they would tell you the sky was blue on a cloudy day, they would tell you a circle was a square. And damned if you wouldn't believe every word, even when the truth stared you in the face. They would tell you they were leading you to heaven, even as you passed the signposts pointing the way to perdition."

Prado stood again. He walked behind the chair, then set his hands on the back. This man had built an impenetrable citadel of imaginations around himself. But he spoke with such certainty, such self assuredness, that there must be a purpose. Had he been sent to test him by the High Masters? Was this man a High Master disguised as a mad man? That must be it.

Prado felt a swell of pride at having uncovered the ruse. He grinned wryly.

"These lies do not vex me. They earn you nothing."

"No," Thomas retorted. "There is a grave difference between what you have been told and what happened. You have simply been indoctrinated by a poisonous misconception meant to strengthen the position of those in power. Such is the peril in permitting a reinvention of history."

"And you will illuminate that difference."

"That," said Thomas, "has been my purpose from the beginning."

## ~~The Past~~ – Redacted

Your Paternos and other figureheads. What do they tell you took place 900 years ago? What do they say triggered the demise of technology, of global connectivity, and the return to isolation and a "fundamental holiness"? Relics are scattered everywhere, are there not? Fragments of the great rock that fell so long ago. Tiny shards of heaven, of retribution. You've seen them, no doubt. Everyone has laid claim to some cracked gray boulder, eroded yellow sandstone, silky obsidian block, a pitted and orange-hued orb, each with different textures and colors. Monuments and altars built to house them. Services to exalt them. No doubt you were astounded by how ordinary they appeared. Just like any other stone, and it must have puzzled you. How could something divine appear so ordinary? Could the world truly be so equitable? And yet, why did they appear so different? The answer is simple: not one is legitimate. Not one.

Even when the answer stares you plain in the face you find a way to ignore it. To accept. Not one came from the original. No surprise, though. Hundreds of years before the sky fell other shrines existed, rumored to house fragments of apostles and prophets and articles of divine significance. People would travel for hundreds of kilometers to see them. To worship them. People would make pilgrimages that served as the culminating event of their lives. A walking stick or a bone or an undecayed finger, or something altogether more grisly. It was a time not altogether different from now. Of course, we came to our senses for a little while. And even though we remained faithful to our respective deities, we weren't fooled by the chicanery of those who would profit from the exploitation of our beliefs and hopes for salvation.

Oh, but the tide has come in again.

Before I begin on what I know, let's review what you know. A quick synopsis of History Standard.

So. The god, or gods, depending on where you are when the story is told, saw humanity had become slothful in their humility, tolerant of vice, of the subtle sicknesses of human nature, and other false religions. As a consequence, and no doubt following deep and deliberate rumination on how best to amend the problem, this god or gods sped a great punishment toward the Earth, to remind humanity of how it ought to behave. That humans were meant to serve The God, or Gods, rather than themselves, and to seek nothing more than to appease the God(s) by worshipping Him/Her/It/Them, maintaining their purity, and destroying the heathens who would seek to harm His/Her/Their people.

Am I right? Yes, of course I am. I've heard it more times than you have, with greater elaboration on different aspects depending on the religion. Once distilled to their most basic components, most religions are indistinct from one another. Strange that you despise one another in spite of your similarities. I suppose the reason is that if you have no enemies, no one to fear and hate, your entire social system falls on its face. It's essential that you identify differences to despise or, if necessary, invent them.

In your particular case the revelation of the purpose for the god's vengeance was delivered in a dream to one Hans Gotte, whom you might recognize as Holy Hergot, or Herr Gotte of Germany. Hans was quite the eccentric in his time. He'd spent time in jail for exhibitionism, and afterwards a few months in a mental institution. I know you've no idea the purpose of such an institution. Suffice to say, your founder was an unstable man who had difficulty maintaining a grip on reality. He also enjoyed attention, and when he found a way to get it, he squeezed it dry.

Even intelligent people forget their senses when desperate and frightened. And the times just before and after the object struck were desperate and frightening times. The idea of any purpose to this horrible destruction, a plan organized by some divine and somehow benign being, and the possibility that this punishment might be mitigated and they could return to their old lives, gave them hope they could recover. That everything might again be as it was without making an effort to rebuild it themselves.

Such desperate fools they were. Desperate and lost. They wandered into the woods and emerged purified. No, not purified. Sanitized. Bleached of their rationale.

As you well know, late one evening Hergot sat in his room. Meditating on the mysteries of the cosmos, straying from one reverent thought to another, when the electricity went out in his building. Without it, the artificial lighting that would have illuminated a building such as the one we're in now failed; communication went from global capacity to mere earshot. Hergot looked out a window and saw the darkness in the streets in the city so far as he could see. Nothing but the stars and moon above, which looked down upon him with disdain.

People gathered in the streets below, carrying candles and battery-powered lights, conferring with one another about the cause of this phenomenon. Hergot intended to join them when his room lit again. So instead he returned to his seat in the middle of the single-room apartment and sat. That's when he heard a deep, reverberating voice utter his name.

*Hergot. Hergot, hear me.*

Alarmed, Hergot leapt to his feet. Spun about. Ready to fight; ready to flee. Eager to be gone rather than investigate further. He spotted someone standing before the window. Outside the city remained dark. In a trembling, flurried voice, Hergot inquired who this person was, how they entered his apartment, what the visitor wanted of him. He feared burglary, assault, or any of the petty crimes people visit upon one another in broad daylight with no fear of punishment.

*I am Jovah. I am your God. I am disappointed in all of you, Hergot. You aspire too much. So I shall smite you. Then, should you be a repentant people, honoring and loving me, you shall have my love in return.*

In a wink, the person vanished. Much as he tried to recall, Hergot could remember no detail, only that he could hear the clear ringing of those words in his head.

Why this account appealed to people I don't know. Timing is my best guess. Hergot surely expected to gain brief attention from the paranoid that would sputter out when his deadline for annihilation came and went unrequited. Yet, to Hergot's great astonishment, astronomers made the announcement of the approach by Apep a few days later.

You don't know Apep? Apep was the name we gave to the "holy stone", as you might call it. A tremendous stone, miles wide. Itself named for an ancient god of darkness and chaos bent on destroying the chief god of ancient Egypt. But we're getting ahead of ourselves.

Hergot was rocketed to celebrity. People wanted to know if humanity would survive. They consulted *him* in their terror rather than those who could best answer questions about the approaching dilemma. I can still see him, starstruck by his own fame, convinced by his own vision and the belief that he'd been selected as a messenger.

His message became the rallying cry raised by the early Paternos. This was their means of gathering humanity to them. And ever since you have been in their grip.

People became penitent. They abandoned their technologies and their modern conveniences. The oceans swallowed up their large cities. Humanity began to war against the evils of their time, destroying those men who would lead them astray. They triumphed. But the fighting did not end there, for there were others who refused to accept the offer of Jovah, and those are the heathens, whose beliefs are so similar to yours, that you nevertheless battle to this day.

That is a watered down version of history. And it is not by any means water tight. Apply the slightest pressure and the entire scheme collapses. Such as the fact that Hergot suffered from severe bouts of schizophrenia or that no such power outage occurred.

I find it fascinating and romantic that the deities choose to work their miracles and revelations through blighted souls such as Hergot. Converting people who would otherwise be considered lost to a purpose so contrary to their nature is a testament to their divinity. But that is where history falters and myth steps in to fill in the holes or put a shine on the murky spots.

Don't misunderstand me. Don't label me an atheist. I very much want to believe there is someone or something watching over us, applauding our triumphs and wincing when we stumble. I am not at war with any deities. That would be utmost stupidity. My war is with humanity—specifically those who manipulate messages from the almighties to bend people to their uses.

The official tale goes that Hergot died during the collapse of a basilica, where he gathered hundreds to pray before Apep struck. For their devotion, Hergot and those he gathered were raised bodily to the heavens when the asteroid struck, shaking the building to the ground, and sparing them the trials that would follow.

Where before Hergot had been made famous, now he was a martyr.

Maybe Hergot did meet a God, and maybe he did receive a message. But did it change him? No. He remained a half-mad egotist feeding his need for attention by blurting a new message from the almighty even after his star had fallen. Rather than being carried body and soul on a cushioned bier to the heavens, he expired unheralded in Amsterdam, in the company of whores who abandoned his bed when they found him lifeless, having poisoned himself by mixing an incompatible cocktail of narcotics.

Even though these myths have been repeated and tinkered with and perfected over the centuries, that does not make them the truth. Truth has all but vanished. Of all the people living today, truth is something that belongs solely to me. Allow me to share it with you.

DeLauder

# Truth

The official version isn't quite in line with your beliefs. The holy stone was forged in the heavens, as it were. Not from justice or some other abstract thought, but rock and ice and metal. The wayward, unused masonry of the solar system.

Let me show you. Here, where the torchlight falls in this loose dirt.

Look here. This is our sun, Sol. Around it are the planets, some sprinkled with their own satellites and insignificant stones. And here the asteroid belt where a great mass of planetary debris is prevented from coalescing by the gravitational forces of the behemoth gas giant, Jupiter. But the stone did not come from here.

Many rocks drift on their own orbits through the solar system, not always in such tidy ellipses as the planets and the asteroids. There is also the cloud of debris, far far beyond the solar system: the Oort Cloud. Every so often a tiny speck is poked from the cloud by a finger of gravity and hurtles toward our sun, swinging back around and into the far reaches again, disappearing for hundreds, even thousands of years. We called them comets. All very simple astronomy. Or so it was long ago. From here, Apep began its descent toward our planet, tumbling along a path that would take hundreds of millions of years to complete.

Many of these rocks were documented, tracked, with the intention of preventing the disaster that nevertheless befell us. But there were so many. And so many millions of calculations to perform. With time, anything is possible. Maybe in another hundred years we might have discerned more than half, or devised a means of detecting and deflecting inbound comets. But this time we weren't quick enough. This time, time ran out.

One unforeseen disaster destroyed everything, and reduced us to a world of pitiful, squabbling zealots.

Somehow we were caught unawares, standing at the edge of so many breakthroughs, exulting in our own greatness. Many blamed hubris for the disaster. Many still do, though most with any understanding knew, with so much debris in our system, it must happen. The only things we didn't know were: When and How Severe.

This Near-Earth Object had gone unnoticed, this dust fragment floating in the mansion of space, one of a billion swinging pendulums in the clockwork of the galaxy. Two weeks was all the time we had—not enough time to save ourselves, but plenty of time to send the world into a frenzied panic.

We determined Apep would strike Brazil, a location you call the Blight, not altogether far from the object that struck the Yucatan peninsula 65 million years ago, leading to radical climate change and the destruction of numberless species in one of the major mass extinctions in our planet's history. Hypersensitive equipment could still detect reverberations from the blow. This blow would not strike with the same force as that which wiped out the megafauna of the Mesozoic era, but the results might not differ if we did not prepare.

After furious recalculations, it was determined the object had been identified long ago, but its predicted path didn't bring it near enough to be considered a threat. Something, somewhere in the blackness of space, had altered its course.

Many took Apep to be the "hand of God" reaching out to smite us in our arrogance, for a lack of faith and excess of hubris, deigning to give ourselves gifts only a God could offer. No thanks to the purveyors of religion whose made it their purpose to evangelize rather than comfort.

But why should a God have anything to fear from mortal men? Why should a God punish creatures he created with so much potential when they tried to better themselves? Would a God ever be guilty of a childish cry for attention?

The Hand of God became a rallying cry, overriding logic and common sense. People prayed, people panicked, everyone blamed everyone else. That was the beginning of the end. Not the event itself. When our faith in ourselves crumbled, that was our undoing. The asteroid was no more than a stiff breeze that blew back the shroud of humanity to reveal us for what we really were.

Some did prepare for the coming blow. Myself among them. We fully expected the world to recover because we had a plan to make it happen. We had the capacity to scrub the skies clean. We could evacuate imperiled locations. We could not stop the impact, and that proved our undoing. We could restore the world, but many demanded preservation, which was impossible. Human beings are visceral and impulsive, even at their expense, and for our failure we earned contempt.

DeLauder

When Apep struck I was high in the mountains, away from the coast, in the country of Tibet—the northern part of the Wicked Lands, as you know them now. In the days and hours beforehand, reports came in of people in churches and mosques and temples and in the streets, gathered in massive crowds, on their knees in prayer. But no amount of prayer would turn this fate aside. It seems strange that people turned on science when it failed them, but didn't turn back when religion didn't save them. Scientists said the impact would strike with the power of a million Hiroshima bombs; that coastal cities and islands would be swallowed up by the oceans; that everything 300 miles from the impact would be vaporized; the dust thrown into the air would create a greenhouse effect, trapping heat, melting ice caps, and keeping those cities inundated by the impact underwater for hundreds of years, maybe more. After the theoretical consequences got around, many millions fled Brazil, and South America altogether, but many millions stayed. Resigned to their fate, perhaps, or confident somehow they would survive. Despite this colossal example of natural selection, the faithful, the fearful, outnumbered those from the Foundation, and other institutions with similar purpose.

It's strange to think that while I was on the other side of the world, when the object struck, I heard nothing, saw nothing of the destruction that would soon unfold. At that moment I thought I felt the ground beneath me shift, as if I'd stepped on a loose stone. A week passed before the dust wrapped across the world and covered us—a great, thick, gray blanket that drew slowly overhead. We lost contact with our satellites, the length of our communications shortened, and our sense of isolation returned, even before everything fell completely apart.

These events served as a hint of the cataclysms to come, sparking a chain of natural disasters. Thin fractures formed beneath the crust for hundreds of miles around the impact, creating volcanoes and vents that vomited sulfur and ash into the air, adding to the debris and creating acid rain that decimated the agriculture. Earthquakes tore our meticulously constructed cities apart, toppling our buildings like dominoes. Tsunamis washed coastal cities into the oceans. The new atmosphere wrestled with itself in search of equilibrium, creating tornadoes and hurricanes and storms of unprecedented power that wrought still more destruction.

Still, the most catastrophic damage we would visit upon ourselves.

The volume and degree of these catastrophes proved difficult for the complex human mind to grasp. It made a perverse sense to believe an angry deity had implemented every tool of vendetta available to them. The trauma of losing an occupation and a social status and a purpose during the mass hysteria leading up to and following the impact for many proved mind breaking. As had the Earth's surface under the hammer blow from the comet, the collective human psyche fragmented. People reverted slowly to their most basic attributes. What people could no longer earn by guile or kindness or payment, they took by force.

Riots began. Everywhere people could gather in large numbers. Anywhere items of value could be found. Force became common currency. Those who could take, did. Those who could not protect themselves or did not join others, perished. It was no surprise. In times of great fear and uncertainty, laws become flimsy barriers and brittle morality crumbles beneath the weight of the survival instinct. A few people tried to maintain the illusion that the old world would continue. Many remained indoors, hoping the fear and desperation and madness would burn itself out like a flash fire. Instead it grew. As more people discovered they were unsafe, or that there was no retribution, more joined the crowds. Pillaging, rape. That's how this new world was born.

We will begin again. That was the promise governments made, but they lacked the strength to be everywhere they were needed, and the longer it took to return to normality, the less people believed and supported, and eventually the powerful governing bodies we knew ceased to exist.

There was little to stop the process. Armies and police forces had disintegrated—most people had deserted to be with their families. Governments still existed, but their manpower had been sapped by desertion, and without their means of control they were no longer viable.

Even so, we served as consultants to those waning governing bodies. Yes. *We*. There were many of us then. Most were much younger than I, but age becomes irrelevant with the passage of time. We told them they needed to restore faith and heart, but even as we told them we knew they were obsolete. And so did they.

From this chaos two entities emerged. The Orders, from which the current theocracies derive, and the Swarm.

The Orders I'm sure you'll have no difficulty identifying. Those maddened looters sacking the cities, driven by fury and desperation, began to exhaust themselves. Until their violence was given new direction by a few religious zealots.

These men and women, the founders of your society, were like any leader before them. They recognized an opportunity to seize power. They reintroduced the idea that the object was a punishment administered to humanity for its cumulative wickedness and a desire to determine its own fate. The only means of absolving themselves was through destroying everything that led them to this state of sin.

They demanded utter abasement, humility, and servitude in order to pacify their malevolent gods. And many, many turned to them—as do most hopeless in search of something to believe in.

They destroyed universities, government buildings, police and fire stations, everything piece of infrastructure that had failed them, and turned their fury on anything the Fathers directed them. They attacked government officials, teachers, businessmen, scientists. Most of all, however, they wanted us.

We were the collective triumph of all those intellectuals. And if they were to defeat and obscure the previous world to save themselves, they would have to destroy us as well.

*Erase the sins of the past, and so doing pave a road to salvation.*

You don't recognize the phrase. It has outlived its usefulness since there is no past to remember, really, only relics to wonder at, and fear.

At the same time the Orders began to organize, as riots became more deliberate and purposeful, focusing their destruction on areas their leaders had chosen, the first Swarm arrived—a final ingredient in the recipe for disaster.

## Swarm

The first Swarm appeared as little more than a large group of rioters, maybe from another faction, but their behavior far outstripped mere riotous destruction, and they did not seem to care which Order to which you belonged. They had a wild appearance to them—unkempt, screaming, slashing at everything that came within reach.

A few people, former servicemen or police men, or civilians, retained firearms and other weapons. So some people were able to defend themselves, and eventually this first onslaught was driven off.

Then came another. This time it was no mere hundreds of people, but thousands. They swept over the thinly populated towns like a plague. No one even knew when the second Swarm struck until survivors arrived to warn us. They were bedraggled and scarred, missing fingers and eyes, gasping their last bloody breaths of life to warn us. For those who survived the onslaught the castles of the old world served to protect them, even helped aid the transition back to a feudal mentality.

By their appearance, they came from the east. Russians and Persians, by their appearance. Then, much later, Indians and Chinese and Korean and more. The Wicked Lands, as you call them, where no one dares venture any longer, not even the brave Crusader Armies. Here the latent effects of the NEO[1] reverberated like the faint tremor of a distant bell. Here populations were high and dense, and the balance between the people and the massive farms that fed them was delicate.

When the debris from the collision pinched the sunlight, crops slacked in their output, and, as a consequence, so did livestock.

Millions starved. But this was a region populated by billions. For those who remained, still greater horrors were to come.

You have seen how fear changes people. Makes them desperate, submissive, impressionable. Hunger changes them as well. Or maybe it reveals them for what they are. Like you, these people became desperate, though their hunger far outweighed their spiritual needs for hope. When manna does not drop the sky for the starving they will not wait for another day, bolstered by their prayers. They turn immediately to their next option. They scavenged, pushing westward, scraping off the remnants of civility as they went.

At the time, I and some others traveled westward, far ahead of the mobs moving behind us, in an effort to support and rally the existing governments and their people. That proved disastrous. The power of the Orders had become surprisingly strong and they blamed the existing government for the current situation, a failure of science to protect them and implying that mere man humanity and its accomplishments could not guard against holy wrath, and they hated us, the products of our science. So, by association, they despised the governments as well. It was, essentially, the end for rule by officials

---

[1] NEO—Near-Earth Object

elected by the masses and became rule by a few within the Order chosen by themselves. But that's not important yet.

More than a year passed before it became apparent what approached from the east, despite our alarms and calls for preparation and exploration. Much of the population had lost contact with one another, divided amongst the land masses, and the unbroken chain of communications satellites provided had been shattered. Infrastructure had been reduced to shambles and most people worked on surviving, which didn't allow much time to determine the whereabouts of anyone else.

In the meantime, the socioeconomic strata began to fracture.

After several months passed with no improvement, the belief that normality would return began to ebb even in those who believed we could help. The need for immediate gratification is something to which most people fall prey. We can't help it. We are finite—we simply don't have time to wait. Those with ample resources, government authorities and the very wealthy, thought Armageddon would end with time and guidance, and they could wait it out, then reassume their positions of authority. That seemed more dubious as time passed, as the Orders gained strength, and as strange rumors of wild unrest came to Europe from the east.

Those without stockpiles of food and water needed other means. Europe and Africa and what remained of the Americas became nations of scroungers. Without resources with which to barter services, the infrastructure upon which the capitalist world was built cracked and foundered. Only those with a bloated sense of justice remained at their posts,    a    few    officers    and administrators, leaving them wildly undermanned and effectively neutered in all but the smallest patches they could oversee. The whole world stripped of governing bodies, of restrictions, of laws, and the personnel to enforce them, those with the most aggressive survival instinct turned on their neighbors. Something new was born out of them in this time. The law of property abandoned, people became governed by a law of survival. People remained somewhat coherent. They could still reason, but reason became a means to an end, not a system that raised ethical boundaries. The weak and empathetic were quickly destroyed, leaving a great many governed by the idea that might made right, and were not easily overcome.

Hunting parties formed. Hundreds strong. They set out for population centers, places where people retained a sense of security, where the wealthy and elite maintained stores of food and a sense of security. The affluent, who were unable to give up their possessions, were the first taken. Government officials, whose wealth was derived from the taxation of its citizens, went next.

I'm sure back then, when people could be divided into fiscal constituencies, haves and have nots, the biblical nature of the selection process would please you. But that did not mean the penitent were saved. Those few places of worship also served as gathering places, and where people gathered the raiders came.

The strange thing about these raids, their interest in the supplies diminished over time, until they no longer seemed to take anything with them. Neither did they leave any survivors.

Do you yet grasp what I'm saying? Perhaps not. Such an atrocity may be beyond even your imagination.

They did not attack for gain; they took nothing. They became feral, loving carnage for the sake of destruction, as a means to satiate a gnawing boredom, an outlet for their energies, and an expression of the genetic roots of man laid bare by the stripped environs in which they lived. More and more they returned empty-handed, perhaps as a consequence of depleted foodstuffs, but I think because they had no need and simply enjoyed the torment they visited upon others, the absence of rules, the freedom from morality. Because that is what many people are, at the heart of them. Hedonists. Masochists. They implement law only when they feared occurring to them what miseries they wished to visit upon others.

When they caught someone they tore them to ribbons like starving hyenas, pulling away clothing, then flesh, then blood and bones until they had reduced the victim to a scattering of rent pieces. Can you imagine being torn apart, living, one piece at a time? Whatever comes free most easily goes first. A finger, or an arm. Not enough to kill you. Death doesn't come until after your skin is peeled away, your chest opened, your vitals strung out like spilled pasta. You never forget those gargling screams. Your public executions make me wonder whether or not the menace has truly been extinguished, or adopted instead.

Deprived of resources once so easy to acquire, there must have been a break, a mental fracture that allowed people to disconnect from their behavior in order to survive. We are excellent survivors. That's how we've existed for so long. But having survived for a while in such a fashion, they must have found the violence a nourishment of another sort, until it was all they craved.

Humans preyed upon other humans, like monsters from some lurid tale of resurrected demons. Desperation makes demons of men. It should have brought people together. Instead, they found it easier to vilify other humans, to hate more deeply. That was just the start, of course. We wondered what they would do with this hatred after they had exhausted their victims, because hatred murdered but could not itself be killed.

Here the Orders stepped in, gaining coherence while harnessing the madness by giving people purpose and direction. They had made strongholds of the old world castles, which allowed them to withstand the ravagers who took and murdered, or simply murdered, and as the only thing similar to a governing body, people fled the raiders and looked to them for aid. So it was the Orders gained greater followings, greater influence, to name themselves. As the Orders took people in, the raiders found fewer pickings, and were themselves absorbed and repurposed.

Thus were formed the Armies of Christo, the Sons of Muhamm, the Jehovite Army, the Armies of Shiva, and many more that were either driven west or crushed by the Swarms, swallowed up by other Orders, or destroyed by more powerful Orders later on.

As these infant Orders gained power and numbers they invariably came into conflict with one another. They had plenty of zealous followers who found protection within the network of structures, purpose in building still more fortifications, and an army of people bent on cruelty the Order that controlled them had no difficulty sanctioning through one divine manifest or another.

Just as several became large enough to notice others, just as their beliefs became known to one another and allowed them to identify their differences, just as the armies began to gird themselves for conflict the first Swarm fell upon eastern Europe.

I remember the first indication I had of an approaching Swarm. I had traveled eastward to evaluate several of the Orders, to determine their level of indoctrination, to see if they had any sense in them or if the members followed the dictates of their leaders without questioning the motives of their supreme being.

Much of the plantlife had perished due to a dearth of sunlight, leaving the land barren and dusty. When wind whipped or a small group of people traveled through the wasting lands one could see them long before they arrived. Their path raised a faint cloud of dust visible for several kilometers. Then must have seen me approaching. Or would have.

As we neared our destination in a stripped down vehicle, we saw a great cloud of dirt above the city of Istanbul, across the Bosporus strait, in what was once Turkey. Before long we began to encounter refugees who fled the city, wild-eyed and frantic, some missing fingers or eyes, bloody and wounded, attempting to clamber onto the frame of the vehicle. Not long after we saw more people streaming through the buildings and up the road toward us. But these people did not appear to be fleeing.

Emaciated and blood encrusted, they came at us at a gallop, howling when they saw us and somehow recognizing us as something other than their compatriots. I never understood what made them seek out victims rather than claw at their own. Such was the pointlessness of their madness, I don't know why they did not exhaust it upon one another. But they shared some bizarre camaraderie, joined to one another with the same thoughtless fervor as a member of one of the Orders. You would claim they were hosting, possessed by a mad spirit of destruction, though I've seen members of your armies in a similar state of blood lust.

We fled, carrying as many as we could, faring better than those on foot, and the Swarm followed. Only long after, after the final battle and several years after, when we were brave enough to venture eastward again, would we discover how significantly that Swarm had been eroded by the defenders holding Rumelihisari castle. The bones heaped in stacks before the walls and at every aperture. A truly terrible and historic battle, utterly unrecorded due to the sheer ferociousness of the combatants.

We warned the next settlement where we arrived, but they scoffed. The divine had raised no such alarms. The refugees did not belong to the same Muslo Order as those from Istanbul and would not grant them entry. Even then, an idiotic sense of otherness prevented cooperation and made a bad situation worse by allowing it to get out of control. We continued on and the Swarm rolled swiftly over them, and on, as indifferent and undeterred as a river along its course.

Only after several weeks did a number of smaller Orders join forces and confront the first Swarm. The fighters of Christo Roma, as they've come to be called, met the Swarm at the ancient walls of Thessaloniki as it moved through Greece, eager to scrap and eager to claim victory for themselves. This army of five thousand encountered a horde of fifty-thousand mindless people who seemed to be ignorant of fear and only mildly deterred by pain or injury. Christo Roma cut the Swarm's numbers in half, which was impressive for a group of undisciplined brawlers who eschewed contemporary weaponry in favor of pikes and spears and swords, and whatever weapons could be had in ancient armories and museums. Most weapons had been mere decoration for hundreds of years.

But for an ounce of foresight, they might have been eliminated rather than merely decimated. As they marched they sent word to neighboring Christo nations to join the Crusade, hoping to gain followers. Fortunately for Roma, the Greeks took up the call, perhaps thinking to reclaim some ancient Hellenic glory. After all, their disparate city states had stopped the Persian armies of Darius and Xerxes thousands of years ago through their military expertise in an era of swords and spears. Why not now, when the world had fallen backwards? Why should Hellas not rise again, asked their leaders. So people gathered, former military and police and soldiers of fortune, and they marched northward. And as the final five hundred Christo Roma hunkered in the White Tower, waiting for the screeching hosters from the east to hurl them into the Aegean Sea, the Greeks arrived, and drove what remained of the host into the water.

So the First Swarm ended, and the power of Hellas was restored for a short time, and Christo Roma greatly weakened. But both would come to an end before long, though not entirely under the crushing weight of the two remaining swarms.

How do I know all of this? I remember. I collate. Of course I was not present during the battles, nor did I follow the Swarms along their path. I didn't have

78

surveillance intelligence or any influence with those in power any longer. What I had was what I'd always possessed: memory and time. When the opportunity presented itself, I explored. I saw the broken tower in Thessaloniki, spoke to the survivors of battles, retraced the steps of those swarms for as far as I could travel without running short of supplies. There's quite a lot you can infer on your own, and what you can infer you'll often discover contradicts what you are told.

# The African Swarm

After the first Swarm the Orders realized their insulation might prove their undoing, so they began to seek out intelligence, sending out scouts and exchanging information with one another. This sort of collaboration led myself and others to hope that we could once again reach a state of relative equanimity and rebuild in a meaningful fashion that could restore our world to a semblance of what it had been.

This hope endured through the destruction of the final Swarm before its final annihilation.

Scouts worked their way eastward and southward, reporting barren cities. Those tracing eastward along the path left by the first Swarm found no human life for thousands of miles. Those traveling south crossed the Mediterranean from Italy to Sicily to northern tip of Africa in Tunisia. They found broken and empty cities there as well, and people began to wonder if the Swarm had spiraled all around them before destroying itself on the borders of Europe.

From Tunisia scouts went east, following the coastline and finding destruction in Libya and Egypt. Others went westward with the same results, until they reached Morocco and, to their astonishment, encountered the rear of a massive Swarm as it approached the strait of Gibraltar.

It took almost a week of travel by land and sea to bring the news of another Swarm, the African Swarm it was called, to the heads of the Orders. And because this Swarm had a name, it made sense to name the initial Swarm, which became known as the Minor Swarm. There was some sense in the title, since it was smaller and first made contact in Asia Minor. Though the real purpose was far more political. Calling the first swarm minor diminished compared to the latter swarms, and gave greater weight to the victors over the final swarms. That, of course, was part of Michael's plan. More on that clever monster later.

At first it was surmised the African Swarm would not cross the straits, that a watch could be placed to ensure it did not circle back towards Egypt, Palestine, Israel, Syria, and pass through Turkey and into Europe again. So the scouts returned, and when they encountered the few people left behind to monitor the Swarm, they discovered it had departed. Not back east, nor south into the heart of Africa, but north, across the strait, like a herd of gazelles crossing a stream in search of fresh pasture. It may be thousands drowned, too exhausted to cross, trampled, or swept away in the current. It's possible nine in ten died as they traveled northward through Africa or eastward across the Arabian desert. Compared to the population demographics, either very few joined the swarm, compelled by whatever force brought them under its sway, or a great many died as it traveled. It's likely the culling from the fording of the Gibraltar strait reduced their numbers to something manageable. Even so, three million came ashore, and scorched northward through Spain like wildfire.

The second swarm was filled with blacks, a dark-skinned African as contrasted with the lighter skin of an Egyptian, so they became a suspect ethnicity, even those who already lived in Europe. Many renamed the African Swarm the Dark Wave, furthering an ironic implication that all blacks had an inkling of the savage and mindless. It came as little surprise that the Orders used the composition of the African Swarm to persecute those with dark skin. Religion, like any cult populated by the vapid and easily indoctrinated, is frequently used to shroud and excuse bigotry.

The African Swarm foraged, not unlike the hunter-gatherers we once were. They did so with abandon, however, destructive in their voraciousness, like locusts, depleting the already struggling landscape. So even those people hidden within the great medieval castles two which many had fled would starve in time, even if they never came under assault. They were effectively under siege. The people of western Christos had to fight or die, or hide and die anyway. Because human beings cling to the faintest possibilities of survival, even in the bleakest of situations, many thousands sallied forth. Not surprisingly, they were summarily destroyed.

These engagements and the presence of food for scavenging slowed the advance of the Swarm, allowing many in the north to prepare as best they could for the assault that would come across the Pyrenees mountains. The remaining Orders with enough strength to combat the coming Swarm, Muhamm, Jehovite, Christo, and some Shivans, drew up their forces in an uneasy truce, and waited.

A month passed as the Swarm swept up and down the Iberian peninsula, eradicating everything it encountered, and pushing the populace before it over the mountains and into France. Your ancestors, I would think, crossed then. Otherwise they would never have survived and returned. Then, when nothing remained to destroy, the Swarm began the slog over the Pyrenees.

The weather on the mountains cut the African Swarm in half, as the armies awaiting them hoped it would. However, a staggering 1.5 million made the crossing intact. Years later, when I had a chance to survey the area where they came over the mountains I found scattered and grooved bones. Never a complete skeleton in one place. The fallen had nourished the survivors, so when one-and-a-half million hosters descended from the peaks into France they were diminished in numbers, but those number were strong.

One of the important things to remember about the Swarms and their encounters with the various armies they encountered is that they did not engage in a typical fashion. If they saw themselves defeated, they did not retreat. They never considered defeat. They fought to the last. And if they saw the forces arrayed before them turn and flee, they pursued. No prisoners were taken. If an army lost to a Swarm it was utterly destroyed.

A battle with a Swarm, when engaged on its terms, was an endless melee. Even in ancient times, where battle lines joined hand-to-hand in a general scrum, armies might have taken a breath. Fighting is hard work. Discipline is important, crucial when taking on a fatigued enemy. Fresh troops meeting tired ranks often proved victorious. With a Swarm no such lull occurred. Wave after wave after wave swept against you until either it was destroyed or the waves carried past the dead bodies of the defeated armies.

This was the opponent the armies of the Orders faced. A terrible one, but not one they fully understood. There could be no truce or negotiated surrender. Destruction of one or the other was the only outcome.

Arrogant and foolish, and ignorant of what they faced in spite of reports from the clash in the east that had all but destroyed Christo Roma, the armies took up independent positions on open ground, confident in the support of their particular deity, so long as they were held in favor, so long as Moses held his arms aloft, they would be victorious. Battles were henceforth never lost due to incompetence, but a lack of faith.

When the Shivan army encountered an arm of the Swarm stretching along the southern French coastline, the faithlessness of its people was proven by the army's rapid destruction. So followed with the Jehovite army. The Christo and Muhamm armies, being far more sensible, fled back to the north.

This is not to say the Shivans and Jehovites did not have some degree of success. They destroyed 3 for every 1 of their own soldiers lost. That amounted to almost cutting the African Swarm in half again.

This doesn't coincide with what you know? Of course not. The armies of Muhamm are said to have turned on the Christo armies in an attempt to seize control of the continent during a time of great duress. It's a convenient revision of history if you don't bother to think about it. History is so riddled with them it's difficult to know which tales to trust. You can trust me, however.

The army of Muhamm was not filled with fools. Not utterly. They knew they could not defeat the Swarm alone. However, the Christo armies needed an excuse for war with Muhamm, a reason to drive out their allies, and this lie suited them well after the Swarm had been crushed at last. And it worked, even on those who knew the truth and lived it.

The retreat north bought time for the armies to better formulate a strategy. They could not allow the Swarm to wander where it would and wait for it to meet them at a point of battle that gave the Christo and Muhamm armies the advantage. But they could not fight in a bottleneck where the forces of the Swarm could overwhelm them with sheer numbers. This was not the army of Xerxes at Thermopylae. This was a stampede, a colony of army ants, with no sense of self, only a compulsion to drive violently forward. So rather than concentrating its forces, a strategy was devices by a Vitruvian whose name you might recognize: Michael.

# The Archangel Michael

Of course, Michael was the name he gave himself, not his true name. General Donald Trumbull, in case you wonder. I don't expect you to remember the name, so Michael will suffice, for the sake of familiarity. Certainly there were many great biblical archangels, though the best way to determine their greatness is to arrange their fall and measure the distance. And Michael fell so very far.

Where I was the first, and a test subject chosen for my ability to remember, Michael was selected for his military knowledge. Michael was almost sixty years old when he entered the program, easily the oldest of us, yet still fit as someone nearing thirty. Such is the nature of the profession, I suppose. Long enough in service to have acquired enough experience to safely comment on almost all military matters, despite existing in a world where military matters were becoming a thing of the past.

In Michael's case I saw one of the Foundation's few errors. I did not see the purpose of granting a man of war extended life to offer advice for a profession in decline. I saw him as a livery stableman at the advent of the automobile industry; a candlemaker as the electric light gained in popularity. Backwards, an anachronism. He didn't like me either, probably because he knew I considered him an error. That belief confirmed itself when he attempted his coup d'état.

Presenting himself to the High Masters of the Christo Order, he introduced himself not as one of the Vitruvian men, but as the archangel of war. He had defeated the armies of Satan eons before, as he claimed; he could defeat this soulless rabble as well in this time of great need when the gates of hell had opened on Earth.

Wise men, even High Masters who robe themselves in the hyperbole of their position but still don't believe it, could nevertheless see the advantages of having a heaven-sent archangel to guide their defense against the Swarm. They did not, however, anticipate his treachery.

Michael had appeared in several historical religious texts: Hebrew, Islam, Christian. He could have offered himself to any of them. Of course, the Jehovite army was destroyed and Michael perceived the Muhamm army as fewer in number in Europe. He simply chose the best army to suit his purpose.

His purpose? To consolidate the Christo Order into an empire that he could rule as a representative of the Sky King. An angel, as he designated himself, sent to lead the Christo Order to salvation through complete subjugation of the world.

Plenty of men like Michael have come before him: Alexander, Trajan, Genghis Khan, Napoleon, Hitler. These came closest to success. Of course, you can attest to the fact that none came so close as Michael.

It's possible his resentment of me led to the extermination of the Vitruvians. He could tolerate no rivals, no similarly gifted humans, knowing we might form a similar cult, and so branded us devils. Who would question an archangel sent from heaven to drive out the demons plaguing the land? He played his hand deftly and effectively. A brilliant tactician, just as the Foundation hoped. And that, I think, was their greatest error—to preserve a feature of humanity we hoped to reduce to irrelevance. His successes and policies cemented the Christo Order's power and furthered its distaste for the secular. He did so to solidify his power, not anticipating its abrupt conclusion. And where one person grows strong and dominates other people, the remainder tend to grow weaker.

How do I know of this plan? He told me. Michael, a trained military man with an abundance of life available to him, was justifiably arrogant. He almost succeeded. I don't doubt he would have, had I not arranged his murder. After all, he was no archangel and all men can be killed, even myself.

But that's a separate story.

Michael reorganized the Christo army, taking a rabble and creating platoons, companies, and divisions, appointing officers with military or law enforcement training. He gave it what an army should have: discipline and organization. It's surprising how quickly these things were lost in the frantic years after Apep struck. Such was the consequence of our reliance on prophets and seers and crooked peddlers of faith rather than professionals who knew their jobs.

Even with his disciplined army, Michael's plan did not include a massive, pitched battle gambling everything. He allowed the Swarm to penetrate deeper, to the alarm of citizens, and disperse into more manageable numbers. Only at bottlenecks did the Swarms accumulate, or where cities crowded against the landscape. Michael chose to attack them at their weakest and least concentrated, encountering hundreds at a time rather than hundreds of thousands.

Reports of victories, little more than minor skirmishes, trickled back to the Order strongholds. One after another after another. Staggering triumphs. Where once the Orders had lost tens of thousands in each lost battle they now lost ten in a week, and often as a consequence of a failure in discipline. The weakest, Michael said, died in battle, leaving only the strong. Every death refined the Christo army, making it more powerful.

He zig-zagged down the western coast of France, then pushed east toward Italy and Switzerland, and crushed the few thousand remaining at the foot of the Alps. The strength of the Swarms was concentrated numbers. With numbers, they could not be resisted any more than a boulder rolling downhill. Without it, nothing more than a rabble easily brushed aside.

The African Swarm was defeated, and Michael made a hero. Though only briefly.

But before that, Michael drove on to the Muhamm army and crushed it, declaring a Crusade against all non-Christo Orders, and starting the intertheologian wars that continue to this day. For while he may have driven other Orders from Europe, they existed or escaped to elsewhere, bringing news of his hostility and hegemony.

When Michael returned from the triumphs over the other Orders, he was again feted as a hero, but this time he deigned to seize control from the High Masters. In a matter of days those who agreed to serve him were reduced to a council of consultants, but who were expected to support and justify his actions. Those resisted were the first High Masters to fall, to be labeled possessed, or hosters as you call them.

The wheels of history had turned in his favor and it seemed Michael had his Empire well in hand. Then came the third Swarm, the Russo Swarm, 15 million strong, that swept over the Carpathian mountains and destroyed a garrison of five thousand heroic Greeks who defeated the first Swarm at Thessaloniki.

# The Russo Swarm

While the High Masters told themselves they had found a general capable of overcoming any enemy, Michael knew the same strategy could not work with the newest Swarm. This time too many had crossed into central Europe intact. Even allowing them to disperse amongst the countryside would not diffuse the mass of enemies to a great enough degree to pare down their numbers.

Michael knew the only thing that could give them an advantage and stave off annihilation was the use of 21$^{st}$ century weaponry, primarily artillery and firearms to replace the swords, spears, and axes to which we had regressed. To this the High Masters agreed, albeit reluctantly and in limited quantities. Michael knew of weapons caches where they could be obtained, and took four weeks to train an elite ten thousand in their use.

In the meantime the Swarm pushed on, following the coastline and buying Michael and the Christo armies more time. It smashed through Greece and back north through Albania and Macedonia, then cut a wide swath along the coast of the Adriatic sea, raking Bosnia & Herzegovenia, Montenegro, Croatia, and Slovenia off the map before turning sharply north, as if sensing the resistance building against it. At this point Michael knew he'd run out of time.

Michael had several divisions in the Christo army now. Many volunteers. Many gathered up by draft. In wartime we accept many atrocities as necessary. We'd all read Orwell. The trick to maintaining control through brutality and fear, to make them seem necessary, Michael realized, was to ensure a constant state of wartime.

He sent four divisions south to meet the enemy, holding the final division in reserve: his elite corps. The ballistics division. Strong, disciplined, loyal, well trained and extremely well armed. Those that went before were naught more than fodder sent to do as much damage as they could. Though they could scarcely be told so.

In all, two hundred thousand fighters were destroyed by the Swarm. They cut down the Russo Swarm by almost two million. A staggering feet by all accounts. Such was their resolve. They seemed to understand their purpose fully, and went to their deaths gladly. Who feared death when a glorious afterlife awaited? But then, if such was the case, why bother to fight in the hopes of allowing others to continue living? Why not embrace destruction and join the whole of humanity in the afterlife? It's that doubt, you see. Even the most devout have it. That infinitesimal morsel of What If?

Still, they met their deaths well, confident in the fact that with each kill they brought the Christo Order closer to victory, and even so with their deaths. For, as they had been trained: "By my death, we become stronger."

This left a staggering thirteen million members of the Swarm bearing down on a mere ten thousand, though a ten thousand armed to the teeth.

## DeLauder

Michael arrayed his troops near Lausanne in western Switzerland on a plateau in the Alps mountains, with the narrow lake Geneva to his south and Lake Neuchatel to his north. Surrounding himself on all sides with natural defenses, he hoped the geography, he expected, would slow the horde and, ideally, allow him to eliminate many en masse as they reached the beach and came down the mountains. If it did not, however, he would be surrounded quickly and destroyed.

Michael had the buildings along the lakefront razed to provide a clear line of sight and had the artillery zero in on the eastern edge of the lake, where he expected many would attempt to skirt around. With luck, the enemy would send much of its force through this keyhole targeted by the powerful, long-range guns.

Luck, as so often seemed to be the case, was with Michael when the Swarm arrived. They came with the first light and passed down the mountains and toward the lake, just as he'd hoped, then began a route around the lake, bunching tightly and making an excellent target for the entire day. In the end, the east end of the lake had overflowed into the craters left by the shelling and bodies tangled in the water like the logjam of a hewn forest caught in a river by the sheer number of floating materials.

With occasional lulls, the story repeated itself through the night and the next day. Sometimes a few hundred would escape the barrage and approach the city, but these were cut down by rifle fire from men in the buildings who were told to hold their fire until the enemy had closed to less than one hundred yards. It appeared the fight would be long, but simple.

By the fifth day the Swarm had only half its original numbers and the stream seemed to slow. Some wondered if the Alps had claimed several million in their crossing. Perhaps the vanguard forces had destroyed more than expected. Those hopes were dashed on the seventh day when, after a day in which a few stragglers stumbled into the city, the great mass of the Swarm arrived as one, streaming toward the city like a great avalanche and stretching far beyond the battle lines of the Christo army.

Michael quickly turned his formation to account for the flanking action, but not fast enough. The artillery, far to the rear of the front, fired many times and exacting terrific damage on the Swarm, but in the middle of the day the guns fell silent. The Swarm had reached them and now wound back around to surround the riflemen that remained.

You know how this battle ends, or a version in any case. So you might wonder how I know how it transpired in such detail. The answer is straightforward enough—I was there. Not willingly, but as Michael's prisoner. As a Vitruvian I was a special prize, but Michael wanted me to live, to remember. That is, after all, what I was meant to do.

Without artillery to thin the ranks for the riflemen, the Swarm drew closer and in much larger numbers. Michael and his elite fighters had gambled on complete victory or complete annihilation. He would get both.

The rapid hosters of the Swarm dropped in heaps, obstructing their own advance with their dead. And still they came on. Michael pulled his forces deeper into the city and collapsed buildings to create additional debris the Swarm would have to navigate. It was a successful ploy, but sheer numbers would be Michael's undoing, and he understood it. He watched as men burned up and jammed their guns from overuse, even though they had been trained to fire in bursts. The volume of humans clambering toward them permitted no relief.

And then, as the defenders pulled back behind yet another wall of rubble, thinned to a final hundred men versus five million, the Swarm relented. Somehow, impossibly, they would survive. The fighters cheered, and Michael wondered what might have compelled them to withdraw. In that moment of surprise he suffered a second shock when he realized I had escaped.

How I got away isn't important to this story. What is important is what I left behind. What Michael in his arrogance did not realize was that I had done some exploring in my time after the fall of civilization when it seemed our existence and aid would not be enough to return us to the way we had been. I went back to where I came from, the Foundation, and found it much the same as I'd left it. Albeit with a few helpful leftovers I've found very useful over the years.

The letup no doubt came as a result of my escape. Humans in a Swarm lacked heightened senses or strengths, perhaps apart from an uncommon stamina that came from an ignorance of one's limitations. Their cognitive abilities sagged considerably to what I would compare to an angry, very anxious pigeon. They were jittery and hostile, and pounced on anything they perceived to be a living being, but didn't do well with problem solving. I could cloak my image, but not the sounds I made in passing nor the effect of my body brushing against things. They heard me leaving, saw blocks kick and roll as I passed, and saw a thin wall of dust raise where I passed, but did not see me and therefore did not know how to respond. Some might have followed, investigating, waiting for me to show myself, and indeed the limitations of that technology, primarily the short duration for which it could be used, almost proved my undoing. I managed, by the slimmest of margins, to slip into the subway system, avoiding the horde, Michael and his remaining men, and the destruction that would consume them all.

For behind me I'd left a nugget of technology not seen in operation for some time: a small, thermonuclear weapon, no larger than my outstretched arm, atop the tallest building I could locate without giving my position away. Despite its size, it was more than enough.

When I vanished into the tunnel, the confusion that had spread amongst the Swarm disappeared as well, and they resumed their attack, crowding inward on Michael's forces. Whether he survived until the end, I don't know. I was several miles into the tunnels when the weapon detonated, obliterating the entire city and turning everyone in it to hot ash.

Your histories say that Michael, his victory won and his purpose concluded, returned to the Sky King along with all his soldiers. That might be true in a sense. Michael never returned from that battle, but he left it as a pillar of ash, and if he ascended he did so as flakes on a plume of warm air.

While this did not end the Swarm, its numbers were insignificant and reduced to stragglers wandering the countryside, identified and destroyed in the fullness of time.

It was the greatest and the last Swarm, the human population having all but exhausted itself. A tiny expeditionary force was created, sent eastward, and returned a year later reporting nothing to be found but derelict city ruins.

In surveying the carnage afterward I discovered the bulk of the Swarm to be not Russian, but of east Asian descent. Chinese and Indian, unsurprisingly. They had the bulk of the population. I traveled eastward along their path and surveyed the horrors they'd visited upon the lands between the Pacific and Atlantic oceans. With exception to what survived the cataclysm inflicted by Apep, almost nothing survived. Certainly nothing human. Burnt empty cities marked a line from east to west like a line of latitude on a globe.

The cause of the Swarms escapes me, as yet, nor why they came in groups rather than stragglers. Perhaps some almighty organized them to test you. But to do such a thing to a human being, to reduce the, to a feral state and send them against fellow humans boggles me. The only thing that makes sense is a general hysteria, a widespread madness brought about by fear. I don't know. I know too little of the human mind to guess what degree of stress is required to drive it to madness. Perhaps the failed attempts at nuclear strikes by India, which caused Apep to carry with it radioactive destructive force, somehow transformed people in mind and spirit, though I don't know how the any of the radioactive debris could have reached eastern Asia and Africa, and not Europe. Perhaps it did, but Europe was possessed of a different sort of madness. But whatever transpired there, many hundreds of millions went beyond a boundary of human thought from which they could never return.

Though Michael was gone, the lesson he taught was not lost on the High Masters. With perpetual war came expanded power. So they manufactured a war. A Crusade. They raised an army, a minor one since that was all that could be spared, and set about eliminating the other Orders. The other Orders, likewise weakened by the Swarms, offered just enough resistance to survive. So the war ground on indefinitely, giving the people something to occupy themselves and giving the High Masters a tight grip on the power they craved.

The crusades have rolled back and forth across the landscape for almost 700 years. Here and there are sprinkled eras of peace, while the enemy catches its breath and surges forward again, driving one nation out of a designated Holy area for a brief moment of solemnity. Back and forth, back and forth, drawing the same exhausted note from the fraying violin strings of history.

War and violence have become our pastime. We have no patience for exploration and adventure.

But of this you know the history already. I'm not hear to repeat what you already know, but to elaborate, and correct the things you think you know.

So here we are today.

## Prado's Analysis

Prado shook his head, head bowed, chuckling. Could this monster possible believe these stories? When he raised his eyes to Thomas, the man was smiling.

"I know what you're thinking," said Thomas.

"What?"

"You're thinking you know my sin."

"Indeed. Hubris."

"Hubris, is it? Maybe so. But not without reason. That's what separates you and I, after all. Reason."

"You are perceptive, I acknowledge it. But it does not alter or assuage your guilt. And it does not change your sentence. God, King of the Sky and Lord of All Beneath, has a plan, and you are not part of it."

Thomas stamped his foot.

"Do you know what hubris is? Hubris is believing you can understand the mind of a creature beyond understanding. It is believing that you hold the key to the vault of salvation and dispense it through public brutality. We wanted to make ourselves better, not supplant any deities. We never intended to challenge anyone for mastery—that's an archaic fable. We never erected a tower of Babylon to incur divine wrath, destroyed men through sheer foolishness, vilified our fellow man for negligible differences, encouraged followers to engage in war to support our beliefs. Anyone who claims to understand the designs of an entity notorious for the creating the architecture of the universe, and best known for inscrutability, is exceeded in foolishness only by his or her followers."

Prado jerked to his feet. It's true that he did not fully know the mind of God. Yet it was a sin to assume others, such as the High Masters, were not in direct communication with the all-seeing lord above. To believe otherwise suggested people acted on their own rather than through a mandate from the heavens. And that meant either the Sky King did not care enough to submit decrees to humanity, or worse, they were acting against them.

"Blasphemer!"

"You have hoodwinked the whole world with religions based purely upon speculation. How do you know *you* aren't the blasphemer? When did the almighties visit you and explain their reasons for anything? Did they visit Hergot the self-aggrandizing lunatic, who didn't remember any warnings until it was too late?"

"Carroll the Pure was visited by an apparition more than 700 years ago, and god explained his reasons for punishing our world. God also gave us our duties, told us to seek out heathens and destroy them."

"Horse shit. Carroll the Pure was a barbarian who led raids on struggling outposts as humanity stood on the brink of extinction. She pillaged cities for their goods, took the hardy and hale to replace those she lost in the raids, raped the inhabitants, and killed those who resisted. She killed others for sport, and when the prisoners ran out she went on another raid, or she took people from her own troop and made examples of them, justifying

101

her actions by creating the commandments by which you still abide. What sort of monster God condones destruction and the proliferation of violence? What irresponsible God creates a species with the intention of destroying it?"

"You are lying."

"I was *there*! I *saw* these things!"

Prado shook his head in disagreement.

"That isn't possible."

"Don't you understand," said Thomas, "you are the descendants of fiends. So are we all. Throughout history, every society that rested upon knowledge was eventually destroyed by feral hordes infiltrating from the outskirts or corrupted from within. Good people were eliminated in each conquest, yet new good people *always* arose, bubbling up through the muck of humanity around them, leaving their society changed. But you never rose above yourselves, because you deny the past and could never distance yourself from it."

"Then why has our society not been crushed by invaders? Why do we successfully battle the heathens on so many fronts? We have not been overrun in many hundreds of years."

"It's not obvious? You persist because you are invulnerable to your enemies. You persist because you are no different than them. This is a world of warring societies. You persist because nothing changes. You remain the lowest common denominator. You eliminate change by stifling anything that promotes it. This facility is a cog in the machine, a randomized safeguard to prevent thought and selecting people to die in order to preserve ignorance. You will never escape it. There will never be a day that you do not live in fear of the beast you have created, comforted by the illusion that you control it, convinced you are not slaves, but free, locked in a dream from which you no longer know how to wake."

Prado's jaw tightened. This man would never admit his guilt, never apologize for his outrageous claims, any more than Prado could turn upon the Sky King. It shocked him that the Sky King did not strike him dead where he sat, though he suspected the Sky King left some responsibility to humanity, offering an opportunity to showcase their judgment and faith. He was damned, utterly, and Prado could not suppress a sense of deep satisfaction that he would be punished eternally for it.

"We're done here," he said.

He walked to the barred door and waved to the guard, who approached and unclasped the padlock. Prado watched Thomas through the bars as the door closed again and the guard relatched the lock.

"We're dying, Confessor," said Thomas. "Humanity is dying out. Surely you can see that. Our numbers dwindle every year. Fewer attend executions. More suffer from disease. We eschewed the vaccinations and precautions to prevent polio and dysentery long ago, falsely believing homeopathic healing could save us, ignoring the possibility that the deity you worship gifted us with the power to heal ourselves. We condemn sexual activity when we need it most and when it is natural. You force us to be unnatural."

"We are natural sinners. It is our ability to be unnatural that will save us. Besides, surely you are not confined by our beliefs to limit your promiscuity."

"Point taken. But even my appetites aren't enough to maintain a population."

Prado shook his head, disgusted.

"Tomorrow you will die, in pain, for each malevolent word you have spoken tonight."

"At last," Thomas remarked. "I commend you, this once, for possessing a form of ambition.

# Parting

Confessor Prado awoke to the sound of shouting and crashing, fearing his room might shake itself apart, still rattling free the last remnants of an interrupted dream.

He'd dreamt he was foundering in a great white light, staggering one way and another until he found a door. When he opened it, the world was full of sound. He could see everything, and it had changed dramatically. The streets were filled with the steady hum of fast-moving vehicles, and on either side great buildings stretched to the heavens themselves, their peaks gutting the underside of low-hanging clouds. The air did not feel hot and suffocating, nor did hissing sand bite at his exposed face. Instead it was cool. Somewhere in the distance he could hear music. In fact, many musics, each from a different direction.

People, thousands and thousands of people, moved along the walkways, bumping and sliding past him like a river around a protruding stone.

Then a tremendous brightness appeared in the distance. He could see it over and between buildings, and people on the walkways turned to observe in wonder. A great black cloud rose up and rushed toward them, and when it struck the buildings they buckled in the middle like stricken animals, and fell.

Prado looked up to see the entire mountain of a building falling toward him, the screams of hundreds of thousands of people ringing in his ears. He dove aside, purely from instinct, knowing he could not outleap this catastrophe, but something held his legs fast. He fell to the ground.

And that was where Prado found himself. Lying on the ground beside his bed, a sheet wrapped about his legs. A dream, he realized. Yet even as he came to terms with this, he realized the shouting continued. It came from within the prison.

Prado tightened his robe and rushed back to the prison cells.

The door leading to the cells reverberated with blows from the other side, as if a brute and terrible beast was trying to bash through.

Prado moved toward the door carefully. Through the small square window he could see hundreds of men and women surging against the exit, screaming and shouting, pounding at the door and walls around it. They could not get out. He felt sure of it.

What had happened here?

Even as he asked the question he already knew.

"Confessor?"

The voice was deep and full of astonishment.

Prado turned to find one of the guards lying by the wall, dressed only in the sparse wrappings of his undergarments. He lay in an awkward position, hands on his back and legs drawn up behind him.

"You did come," he said. "Like he said. I didn't believe at first, but now I do."

"What are you doing here?" asked Prado.

The guard convulsed furiously for a moment, then stopped, gasping.

"I can't," he said. "I can't get up."

Prado moved closer and saw the guard's wrists and ankles were held together with heavy cord. The prisoners continued to pound against the door and wall. He knelt and pulled at the knots, but they would not come free. The hogtied guard would have to be cut loose. But not here. The booming against the door had an ominous, murderous feel, and he felt unsafe.

Prado looked closer, and saw a pillow beneath the guard's head.

"He left you this?"

"So I wouldn't scratch up my face, he said. Can you believe it?"

Prado looked about and found a wheeled table. With an effort he heaved the massive guard onto it and began to wheel him down the labyrinthine hallways toward an exit.

"What happened?" asked Prado.

"That's just it, Confessor. I'm not even sure."

"Tell me what you remember."

# Recollection

It was the shouting that woke me. They always make a pitiful racket through the night. It's something you get used to. Like the smell. The weak light. This was different. You could feel it right off. There was excitement in it. Almost crazy, like at morning execution in the city center.

So I step out through the dorms to the main chamber, club in hand. Might have to mash some skulls to get it settled down again. They're like dogs, and violence is the only thing they understand. It's late, I can't see much. Smash my foot on the door frame that any other time I would have gone around. I'm tired. I'm irritable. I'm looking for something to beat on.

First thing I see when I gimp into the main chamber stops me dead in my tracks. That man, that devil wizard of a man, out of his cell somehow, standing in the center of the whole place inside a ring of blazing torches. Looking up and turning around with his arms stretched out, calling to all the folk in the cells around him. And they're going crazy like monkeys with a burning branch tied to their tails.

I stare at him a bit, not sure how long, mouth hanging open, wondering how in flaming christo he's gotten free. All the while he's waving his arms like he's the prince of Paternos and slinging the sanctified blood of sinners into the crowd, and them people screaming to beat down the walls.

What you think you're doin'? I shout at him. I don't expect him to hear me for all the noise. But he does. Turns about and fixes me with this look of disappointment. Not because he'd been caught, mind you. He says how *unfortunate* it can't be the Confessor. Yeah. You, Confessor. He was hoping it might be you. Didn't say why. But he said I would serve well enough.

I don't know what he's up to, don't care to know what he's up to, but I realize this has got to end right here, so I raise my club and go at him. Little chance of him standing up to me, I think. He's a full head shorter, thin as a rail. I only hope he doesn't run so I can get a good swing on him rather than chase him around. Ran through that ring of fire and swing like to knock his gourd clean off and make a cherry blossom against the far wall. But I miss. Not sure how. I didn't pay much attention to what happened, but remember feeling surprised there was no resistance. One second he's there, the next he's gone, and I'm stumbling through the space where he'd been. Almost fall and knock my own gourd in. So I turn around, swing again, more careful this time, and he just glides away, like it was nothin' at all.

You believed I was helpless, he says. You believe the scope of human ability is something compact, limited by a deity who desires no more than abasement and derives pleasure from ceaseless hostility. How easily you let yourself be deceived. Did your deity tell you that themselves? Or was it delivered word of mouth from someone who spoke to them? Or better yet, someone who spoke to someone who claims to have spoken to a god. Has your religion been modified by the whims of the situation?

I've got no intention of missing the little cuss this time. And I take a swing to knock in god's own teeth. He slips aside, just like before, slick as wet soap, but moves back just as quick with his fists up. One-two-one-two, right in my face. Next thing I know I'm on my back, wondering where I am, and he's got me trussed up with the cord used to ring the noon bell. And it's cold. Real cold. I start to wonder if he's poisoned me, or worse. He looks a bit different now, clothed in a shirt and robe that look a bit big on him, with the clenched-fist patch on his shoulder. It's my uniform, and I'm left with just an undershirt.

That made me mad, as you might expect, so I struggled to get at him, shouting every profanity I could think of. Mohamm this and Jesu that. Invented a few more for good show, but it didn't matter. He just watched, amused, I guess.

Now, he says, if you're done, I have something to show you. All of you.

Most everybody has got real quiet. I can see a few who are close to torches, staring with a half crazy glint in their eyes. All the fear they had, that kept them balled up in a corner or stretching through the bars, is gone. Lots are looking down at me. There's muffled shouting in the distance, people yelling to be let out. I wonder where the other guards are, why they aren't helping, and it occurs to me that it isn't prisoners calling for help, it's other guards trapped in their rooms. I'm the only one to get out. Or rather, he left my door unlocked. He *let* me out. That's when I start to feel scared. That's when I realize he's got a plan.

112

Meantime he stands in the torches and starts talking again. I don't catch much because I'm trying like fury to get loose. My club is real close, and I'm thinking I might need it soon, for defense against any prisoners he might set free. He left it there, I think, just to have fun with me.

Anyway, he's talking the whole time, and on the floor, struggling, not paying all too much heed. But I do pick up on a few things. Strange stuff. Lots of stuff that didn't make sense. Some bits about how they was all prisoners. Not just in here, but their souls, too. And how he could set 'em free. Make 'em masters of their own selves. For always. That they needed to stop being afraid, because it was fear that made them prisoners.

The desiccated form of the leviathan lies all around us, he tells 'em. We make no efforts to return to our own world. We have become acclimated to the landscape. We have made this our home when we owe ourselves so much more.

Do you wish to be set free? he asks. Nobody says anything. The whole place was filled with silence, if you get my meaning. Silent, but there was the noise of thought. Not something you hear, I guess, but you can feel it. Then he says, Let me remind you of what you were, and what you can be again.

He wanders off for a bit and I hear this click, and a kind of humming noise as from some giant insect. It frightened me a bit, because I didn't understand, and I wanted to know. I felt I could handle the fear if I understood, you see. Then far overhead I start to see a few glowing bars strung out across the ceiling. A whiteness comes from them, and soon the whole place begins to get brighter, filling in the gaps between torches so you can see black soot staining the walls above the fires, prisoners gaping across the gulf at other prisoners, as if unaware there was another wall of cells facing them. Every one of them shares the same look of wonder, probably have the same look on my face, but there's no time to ask questions.

A voice booms through the chamber—not the man who spoke to the prisoners. It was brighter, somehow, full of thoughtful pauses. Something snapped, and the lights overhead dimmed, and then there was a man, bigger than any man ever was. He hovered in the air in the opening between the two walls of cells, walking, but not moving. There was a sound of rolling ocean, and we could see giant waves breaking along a rocky shore, and him talking the whole time. We stared a while, trying to understand what was happening, so long we didn't listen to what he was saying for a few minutes. That's what I think he thought was important. It was the words, not that ancient technology.

Funny, my memory isn't the greatest. In fact, if you were to tell me something right now, how to perform one of your rituals for the confessing, I know I would forget in just a few minutes. But what he showed us, the words they used, I can still hear them. There was a... a... resonance to them. An importance. I don't think I'll ever forget.

It wasn't until the image was of the man's face, just his face, that I started paying attention to what he said. After I started listening it was as if the words were being scratched right across my brains.

*The size and age of the cosmos are beyond ordinary human understanding,* he said. *Lost between somewhere between immensity and eternity is our tiny planetary home, the Earth. For the first time we have the power to decide the fate of our planet and ourselves. This is a time of great danger, but our species is young, and curious, and brave. It shows much promise. In the last few millennia we have made the most astonishing and unexpected discoveries about the cosmos and our place within it. I believe our future depends powerfully on how we understand this cosmos in which we float, like a mote of dust in the morning sky.*[2]

The sound crackled and the images of the coastline shivered, then vanished.

Then there's two men talking, one seated in a box, the other one standing. The one in the box is bald and sweaty. His lower lip juts a bit. He seems nervous. The other fellow has silver hair. They're arguing about something, that's easy to guess, but about what I'm not quite sure. The whole situation is drawn up kinda like an execution, but without all the mewling and cries for help.

*We must not abandon faith!* says the bald one in the box. *Faith is the most important thing!*

The silver-haired fellow says right back, *Then why did God plague us with the capacity to think? Mr. Brady, why do you deny the one thing that sets us above the other animals? What other merit have we? The elephant is larger, the horse stronger and swifter, the butterfly more beautiful, the mosquito more prolific. Even the sponge is more durable. Or does a sponge think?*

The bald one, the one he calls Mr. Brady grins at that question, and I have to say that I might too, in the same situation.

*I don't know,* says Mr. Brady. *I'm a man, not a sponge!*

*Do you think a sponge thinks?* asks the silver-haired man.

---

[2] Carl Sagan's *Cosmos*, 1980

DeLauder

*If the Lord wishes a sponge to think, it thinks!*

At this point I have to agree with Mr. Brady. All this talk about sponges and thinking sorta confuses me, but Mr. Brady makes sense. And it's good to know he's made the Sky King his master, as he's master of everything under that sky. At least, that's how I thought at first.

*Does a man have the same privilege as a sponge?* asks the silver-haired man.

*Of course,* says Mr. Brady.

Of course, I think. Of course a man has the same rights as a sponge. More, probably. We've been given legs for walking, mouths for talking, and all manner of other gifts that make us so much more than a sponge. What can a sponge do that we can't? What is a sponge permitted that we might envy?

Then the silver-haired man turns and points to another fellow, seated close by, spindly and meek looking, like any one of our prisoners, and shouts.

*Then this man wishes to have the same privilege of a sponge! He wishes to think!*[3]

It's then I realize it's the fellow being pointed at who is on trial, for, I'm guessing, thinking. It must have been a crime then, too. And I wonder to myself, if it's okay for a sponge to think, why is it not okay for me, or you, or anybody else to think? If thinking is what we do best, why can't we do it? What would happen if other things, like birds,

---

[3] *Inherit the Wind,* 1960

116

weren't allowed to do what they did best? They'd die, wouldn't they? They'd give up their sole advantage and be gone.

That thought really jars me. *What if we've done that to ourselves?* What if the devils we fear aren't the ones trying to get us to think, but trying to trick us into not thinking? Right. What if they found what was best about us and took it away? That would be a triumph of the sort the Paternos always warn against. And, surprising myself, I get a little scared. Didn't think I was so easy to trick and a bit frightened now that I can see through it.

Another click, and the images are gone. I'm looking around, wondering what's going to happen next when I hear something else. A metal clanking and sliding overhead and all around, and realize one by one the cage doors are sliding apart. The clanking comes from broken links clattering on the floor as the doors jerk them apart like grimy old fabric. That's when he came hustling back, and looked down at me with his face flushed and grinning, all full of the devil's mischief.

We should go, he says, then reaches down and takes hold of my shoulders. They're not likely to be friendly with you.

And he drags me out into the hallway, shuts the door behind him, and turns to some rusty panel on the wall. Suddenly the lights go out again. Like magic, and him some bloody wizard.

This will hold them, he says, but not for long. The generator will keep the electricity running for a short while, but when it cuts out the locks will release. Only a few people had the presence of mind to step out of their cells when the doors opened, but the chains are broken, and once the generator runs out it won't take long for them to figure out there's nothing keeping them. Confessor Prado will be here soon. Be sure to tell him what you've seen. I'm sure it will interest him. I leave it to you now. These people are still your prisoners. They cannot escape this facility, but their minds are fired with the hope of being set free. Can you accept the change that must come? Or will you sacrifice, as others have, that last shred of yourself in order to prolong the ruination of our species? Choose carefully.

Then off he goes. Not long after, you showed up, just like he said. And here I am, like he left me, sacked up like so many potatoes.

*Millennium Man*

# Resolution

What would the world be like if humanity was freed from the "shackles of religion." Independent, free to pursue any vice, or develop great things as had once been seen in the world—those crumbling monoliths that stood out of the ocean where cities had been. What greatness might they achieve? A unified sense of purpose in science might remove the need for executions and penitence, and Prado would no longer have to oversee this maddened lot of clawing, yowling animals.

The story made his skin prickle as he wrestled with the knot binding the guard's arms and legs together. It was tight, with two long strands winding out of the great ball. Something in his mind clicked as he worked against the knot. Unsure why, he gripped one of the strands and drew on it. To his astonishment the knot unraveled itself and fell away.

"Christo's holy trousers, my arms," said the guard, who rolled off the table and onto his feet. He stood a moment, massaging his shoulders and stretched his legs, then headed back the way they'd come.

"Where are you going?" asked Prado.

"What? Back," the guard answered. "Can't leave the other guards in there."

"We don't have time," said Prado. "The prisoners could be set loose at any moment. We have to alert the militia."

The guard hesitated. Of course he didn't realize the catastrophic effects of releasing these people. Of returning them to society changed as they were. Touched by the influence of the devil.

"What?" the guard repeated.

"We're going," said Prado.

"But what are we gonna do about all those people?"

"Burn it. We burn the whole thing."

The guard did not move.

"But the people in there. You don't mean to kill them all. Without even their confession."

"People who were going to die at execution," Prado replied. "We will burn this place. Burn it to a pile of smoking ash."

"Guards, too, though. They've done nothin' wrong. Why should they be burnt up with the others? They're my friends. They have families, lots of 'em. What do we tell them? How do we tell them we burnt 'em all up, without a single thought otherwise?"

"We tell them they were sinners, too. Mindwashed by the devil's blasphemies. We tell them they had gone mad, and we, we prevented an outbreak of that madness. You know it's true. Everyone is a sinner. Everyone. Somehow or other."

The guard's eyes grew wide.

"That means you and I are sinners, too. By rights, we should stay to burn up with them."

"Yes. In a manner of speaking."

"We should burn up everybody. The whole world. We shouldn't even be here. Living, I mean. If all people are sinners. Why are we living, then?"

"We will have preserved our society," Prado explained. "These people have been… infected by a zealotry for freedom from God. We must scour that infection. We must scorch the earth where that seed took root."

"That's not right," said the guard. He looked at Prado in confusion, weighing two thoughts against one another. "We can't kill all those people. Even the innocent ones. What if we give them a chance to make it up? Can't we do that?"

"And permit them the opportunity to spread their infection through our community? Never!"

The guard stiffened. His eyes narrowed, giving Prado a hard look. Then, with a sudden movement, spun back toward the door.

"I won't let you," he said.

Prado followed him. Followed him back down the hallway, and back to the door, which the guard began to pull at in futility. He walked toward the gray panel he'd described the devil man using to lock the doors and pulled it open. Inside were a number of black knobs and switches with numbers by them. He reached tentatively toward one and flicked it.

Far in the deep part of the cell chamber a light grew. Many of the people clamoring at the door stopped to look at it. The guard flicked another switch, and another light sputtered to life in the distance. He reached for a third, but never flipped it. Instead, his body slapped against the wall and slid to the floor.

Prado stepped back, observing his work. He dropped the heavy metal bar in his hand.

"So," said a voice from behind. "You've chosen to sacrifice your own humanity. Once again the power to change everything rests in the hand of one person, and that person denies everyone."

Prado turned, glaring into the deep recesses of the chamber.

"Show yourself!" he cried.

"I'm here."

The voice caromed around the room, coming from everywhere.

"I will destroy you."

Prado stalked toward a dark corner, but found nothing.

"You had your chance and you did not. Why? Because you were curious, yes? You wanted to see what I could do, what you knew I would do. As I want to see what you will do."

"Why don't *you* free them?"

"So their fate concerns you after all. Good. Why didn't I set them free myself? Because it must be you. If I do it, it means nothing. The 'devil' release the prisoners? No. That would be too easy to undo. Too easy to condemn. It must be you. It must be someone they respect. It must be one of their own who chooses a different course."

"What course?"

"I don't know. Free these people, see what happens. See if their story spreads. See how people react to an alternative to the present world. Or you can destroy them. You can save your theocracy, but will have preserved it through an act of wickedness. And that wickedness will taint the mission of your society still further. You will be a part of that wickedness. And even though you might have preserved this society a little longer it will have died for you, and your deeds will eat at you forever. Keep in mind, if you wait too long they will find a way to escape on their own, so you must decide soon."

"An act of wickedness? No act to preserve our society is an act of wickedness!"

"Even killing innocent people, like your guards? Like those who have not had a proper confession to expunge their sins before death?"

"What should I do, then?"

"Think, Confessor. Think. That is all anyone must do."

"I can't. I can't think!"

"You are not a bad person, Alejandro Prado. Merely misled. They can hide things from you, but they cannot steal your conscience. Because of that, you know what to do."

"No I don't! What? What is it?" Prado cried, half imploring, half cursing himself for begging the devil for aid, cursing himself in full for not knowing on his own. He wished he weren't in this situation. Wished he'd slept through the whole thing. Wished the building had burnt down around him or been swallowed up by the earth. Wished the guard had killed Thomas yesterday. "What should I do?"

"I know you, Alejandro Prado. I know you miss the children who were taken away from you to go and die in a stupid war. I know you long to mourn in public the wife you mourn in private because she was brought to a place like this. Yes. Your wife was in a place like this, taken from you for reasons neither of you could know, but forced to an absurd confession all the same.

I know you know that innocent people are sentenced to death here. I know you hoped to be something greater than a Confessor, but this feudal society gave you no other option. I know you want to set yourself free. I know you have wished for this chance. I know you have the will to outthink the way they have programmed you. A Confessor must be intelligent to convince people they have gone astray, even when they have not. But that intelligence makes them vulnerable. To questions. To the truth. And that terrifies you more than anything, doesn't it? The truth you know is there, but the great monolith of your faith blocks your vision."

Prado walked to the door where the men and women pressed themselves against the tiny window, showing him their wild eyes.

"Help us!" they cried. "Help us, please!"

Prado backed away from the door, then looked to the panel where the guard lay slumped against the wall. He could not release these people. What if they told everyone they could escape execution? What if they told everyone the wonders they'd seen? What if they told everyone they didn't have to be afraid of their god anymore, that their god wanted them to succeed?

Prado shivered, feeling a sense of ambition and hope touch him as well.

"Get out of my mind!" he shrieked, crouching and pulling at his hair.

Destroying this place would mean taking the lives of not just those sinners in the cells, but of the trapped guards, and the men and women who tended the corridors by replacing torches and laying fresh straw. But to do nothing was as bad as releasing them, because it was surrender.

However, the thought, one avenue he hadn't considered until now remained. One which even the Vitruvian devil may have overlooked. Prado straightened, his eyes wide in the half darkness. One avenue would steal away this devil's victory and the gnawing Prado felt inside himself.

Prado dashed from the room to the nearest doorway. A dim silhouette of the word Exit hung above it. He raced up the staircase, following the coiling stairs, breath tearing at his lungs until the steps exhausted themselves and he found himself on the roof.

Overhead the stars were still and cold, casting a quizzical gaze upon him, wondering what he would do next.

There was no time to think. Any amount of thought would open a window for the devil's influence to enter. So he ran, straight ahead, robes flying out behind him. They slowed him, so he flung them away. He ran as hard as he could, unfettered now, faster than he'd ever moved before, like a beam of holy light searing the blanket of darkness, feeling a fire in his lungs as though they might burst into dust like the heathens' bodies that dissolved into a gray heap after being burnt at the stake. Then he reached the edge, and for a split second stared down at the great emptiness beyond, the broken rocks somewhere in the darkness below, and leapt.

For a moment Prado floated in air, and the idea occurred to him that angels might swoop down and bear him away to a place of glory and recognition for this great triumph. But then he felt gravity take hold and his body tumbled forward through the air, gaining momentum as he approached the earth, and he knew his salvation would come by less spectacular means.

A few instants remained to him, and in those moments Prado's purity remained untarnished, with exception to the faintest needle of pride that penetrated the armor of his faith. In his last moment Prado could not help but suppress a smile, delighted and heightened by the knowledge that he had saved his world, guarded his faith to the end, and that a mortal man in the service of god could and had defeated the plans of the devil.

## Begin Again

Thomas crouched among the jagged fragments of cinder that ran along the rear of the prison and looked down at the shattered body of Alejandro Prado, the giant lamps around the prison illuminating the land for fifty yards beyond the edge of the structure and throwing Thomas' shadow across the rocks with the broken Confessor. A faint smile touched the Confessor's lips, suggesting he had, mercifully, suffered an abrupt death. Thomas hoped his last thoughts were pleasant, and that somewhere in the firmament he'd been accepted into a greater plane of existence for, if nothing else, his unshakable loyalty.

Not far away he could hear the shouts of prisoners fleeing into the arms of approaching soldiers who had seen the brightness of lights and flood lamps flash to life in the structure from miles away. Even now they remained blissfully naïve. It might be comical if it weren't so tragic.

"We were saved!" they cried. "Saved by the devil!"

One by one they were cut down as they entered the ranks of soldiers. Soon their escape and celebration turned into a panic. One by one they were caught and destroyed.

Thomas looked back to the body of the Confessor and frowned.

"So," he said, straightening. "We choose extinction."

Perhaps he too should destroy himself, fling himself from a rooftop and fly to the spirits rather than linger here in a world where he had no place. Return to all those faces and memories chiseled into the rock face of his mind, long gone, each leaving an empty ache where they'd taken space within him. He'd considered it many times before, when his purpose bore down upon him with the weight of humanity. Death was a frontier that always held a distant fascination, and he wondered where it might take him, or if he would exist beyond the point of termination to have the question answered.

Even as he considered he knew such exploration would have to wait.

"The easy path," he murmured, "is not why they chose me."

Prado had perished to defend his beliefs. So Thomas knew he must live in order to save everyone from them.

Overhead the stars winked at him, a billion points of light cast across the canvas of night like a handful of pebbles. Long ago humanity gave the stars shapes, guided their ships by their arrangements, found their place in the world, looked to their designs for comfort as evidence of the divine. A billion billion shapes and arrows and directions layered atop one another like transparent maps, obscuring their message, hiding their paths in the criss-crossing of numberless routes. It would take a millennia to explore them all, a thousand years or more to find the correct one.

Thomas inhaled the cold night air and listened as the cries of the prisoners diminished, their numbers quickly fading, eyes fixed on the stars as they crept across the sky. One thousand years was coming to a close.

DeLauder

"So," he said to himself, "we begin again."

Reluctantly, Thomas' shadow merged with the darkness and he was gone.

## Author's Note

This book has no pictures, which is really a disastrous beginning for a graphic novel, as this was meant to be. Initially, I began this story as an overview for a larger work, suggestion many of the scenarios mentioned in brief would be fleshed out in greater detail elsewhere and from a first-person perspective. My wife, for her part, seemed to enjoy this story very much and insisted that I publish it. I resisted. So she switched tactics, suggesting I try publishing it as a graphic novel. Again, I resisted, since that is my nature, but I found a graphic novel template and plugged in a few scenes, and the world leapt vividly to life. I knew the graphic novel was the medium this story should take.

Alas, I cannot draw, which put a rather large crimp in my designs. My drawing skills have made no significant advances since I was a child who could also not draw.

With that in mind, it would seem an absurd undertaking to conceive of a plot best told in graphic format. Engaging in a project requiring a particular skill necessary to complete said project has never prevented me from pushing forward. So here it is. I still hope to see this as a graphic novel someday. I still hope to flesh out what could be a long, broad story that touches upon more than the topics addressed here, such as the stain of dubiousness set upon any holy law when delivered by people to others. Perhaps I will someday be gifted miraculously with an ability to transcribe the images in my head onto paper. Perhaps I will someday be gifted with someone who can do so for me.

I'd prefer to get them to you directly, but in the absence of these miracles we have this print version that requires you to translate the words into images yourself. I apologize in retrospect for the quality of these images if they came out poorly. Of course, if you're reading the Author's Note first, I apologize in advance.

The reason this story comes to you in this admittedly pictureless form is the consequence of my wife, mentioned here and in the dedication, who demanded I put this out, posthaste. Because I trust her, here it is. For better or worse. Or, perhaps more appropriately, better and worse, because she enjoys the tale so much. Hopefully you will as well, despite the lack of pictures.

You're welcome. And I'm sorry.

Made in the USA
Monee, IL
05 March 2024

54531937R00079